# NIGHT RAID

The sound of footsteps in the night jerked Skye Fargo instantly alert. His big Colt was out of his holster in a flash. Then he saw who it was.

"Damn, what are you doing here, Betsy?" he said. "You could've gotten your blonde head blown off."

"I knew you wouldn't shoot at shadows," Betsy Cobb said. "You're the alert kind, not the nervous kind."

"You're going to outsmart yourself one of these days," Skye grumbled.

"Not tonight," Betsy said, as she dropped to her knees beside him and slowly ran her hand down the smooth nakedness of his chest, and downward over his flat stomach.

Betsy wasn't out to get her head blown off. She was after a different kind of explosion—and she knew just how to get it. . . .

# THE TRAILSMAN 61

# BULLET CARAVAN

by

## Jon Sharpe

A SIGNET BOOK

**NEW AMERICAN LIBRARY**

*PUBLISHER'S NOTE*

This novel is a work of fiction. Names, characters, places, and incidents either are the product of the author's imagination or are used fictitiously, and any resemblance to actual persons, living or dead, events, or locales is entirely coincidental.

Copyright © 1986 by Jon Sharpe

The first chapter of this book previously appeared in *The Wayward Lassie*, the sixtieth book in this series.

SIGNET, SIGNET CLASSIC, MENTOR, PLUME, MERIDIAN and NAL BOOKS are published by New American Library, 1633 Broadway, New York, New York 10019

First Printing, January, 1987

1  2  3  4  5  6  7  8  9

PRINTED IN THE UNITED STATES OF AMERICA

# The Trailsman

Beginnings . . . they bend the tree and they mark the man. Skye Fargo was born when he was eighteen. Terror was his midwife, vengeance his first cry. Killing spawned Skye Fargo, ruthless, cold-blooded murder. Out of the acrid smoke of gunpowder still hanging in the air, he rose, cried out a promise never forgotten.

The Trailsman, they began to call him, all across the West: searcher, scout, hunter, the man who could see where others only looked, his skills for hire but not his soul, the man who lived each day to the fullest, yet trailed each tomorrow. Skye Fargo, the Trailsman, the seeker who could take the wildness of a land and the wanting of a woman and make them his own.

*The Nevada Territory, 1860,
east of the Shoshoni Mountains,
where most trails led to an
arrowhead tombstone . . .*

# 1

He snapped awake and lay very still. He listened, hardly drawing a breath. The sounds came again. Soft sounds: dry grass rustling, leaves being brushed back, loose dirt being moved . . . susurrant sounds.

They would not have wakened most men. But he was not most men. He was the Trailsman and his senses were those of the wild creatures, his hearing that of a mountain cat, his eyes able to rival the red-tailed hawk's. As he listened, the sounds came once again. Something moved through the little glen where he'd bedded down for the night. No deer, he grunted silently, the pauses not those of a deer. No badger or marten. Low enough to the ground but they couldn't help scurrying even when they prowled. No white-footed deer mice. They'd disturb only grass and he heard leaves being brushed. And certainly no bear. You could smell bear a hundred feet away.

Slowly the big man raised himself up on one elbow and peered through the night, his lake-blue eyes narrowed. The thick overhanging branches let only a thin filter of moonlight in, but he found the shape crawling through the underbrush to his right. He remained motionless as he saw a fedora pulled low, dark clothes, a face hidden from view. The figure halted, turned on its belly, and started to crawl toward the Ovaro. The magnificent black-and-white horse was tethered but a few yards away and Skye Fargo shifted his weight as the figure halted only a few feet from the horse, paused, pushed itself to hands and knees. It rose and he saw a slender man step toward the horse. Fargo waited a moment longer until the dark shape reached the Ovaro and started to pull the big Sharps carbine from the long rifle holster hung from the saddle.

"That's enough," Fargo snapped out as he leapt to his feet, the big colt in his hand. The figure froze in surprise, the rifle half-pulled from its holster. "Let go," Fargo ordered, and the figure remained motionless, hands still on the butt of the rifle. Fargo fired a single shot aimed to graze the top of the fedora and he saw it snap off a piece of thin branch that almost rested on the hat.

The figure let go of the rifle, dropped low, and dived sideways into the brush. Fargo holstered the Colt as he darted forward, saw the man roll in the brush, come up on his feet, and run. Fargo increased the stride of his long legs as he saw the man was quick, racing through the trees with sharp, darting motions. Fargo dug heels into the soft forest floor and closed the distance quickly. The would-be thief threw a quick glance over his shoulder, saw the big shape on his heels, and darted to his left, swerved to the right, then left again. Fargo refused to waste time and plunged forward until he was almost abreast of the man; then he spun and reached out with a long, sweeping motion. But the man's reflexes were quick, he ducked low and twisted away to race forward again.

"Damn," Fargo muttered as he followed.

The smallish figure ran straight, dodged between saplings, but Fargo's long legs caught up in a half-dozen driving strides. He saw the figure glance back again, but he was ready, his body tensed, as the man tried to swerve once more. Fargo dived, met the swerving movement with a flying tackle, and went down with his arms wrapped around the man's legs. He hit the ground with his quarry, saw the fedora fall off and a shock of short-cropped, blondish hair tumble loose. The form in his arms twisted free as he frowned, relaxed his grip, and pulled away just in time to avoid raking nails aimed at his face.

"Goddamn, a girl," Fargo muttered, cursed again as he rolled away to avoid the kick aimed at his face.

As the boot grazed his head, he reached out, wrapped one arm around her leg, and yanked. She came down hard on her rear with a yelp that combined anger and pain. He leapt to his feet and saw her turn, try to get up speed to race away again. He reached out with both hands, caught her by the shoulders, lifted, spun, and slammed her back against a tree trunk hard enough to make the breath come out of her with a whooshing sound.

"That's enough, dammit," Fargo snapped, and she stood plastered against the tree trunk, trying to get her breath back.

He peered at a face covered with mud and grime, the short blond hair matted, mud-caked leaves plastered through much of it, shirt and Levi's torn and covered with dirt. She glared back at him from under the caked grime on her face. "Why were you trying to steal my rifle?" he asked.

"To blow your goddamn head off," she flung back.

"Why?"

"You know damn well why," she spit at him.

"You're certainly a hell of an unwashed little thing," Fargo said. "Why'd you want to blow my head off?"

"You know that, too, damn you," she snapped.

"I don't know what you're talking about," Fargo said.

"The hell you don't," she glowered.

"I don't. You've got something all wrong. Who are you?" Fargo asked.

"Don't put on an act with me. It won't work."

"No act. All I know is you look like you've been under a rock for a week," Fargo said.

"Two days, and you know it," she said, her voice rising angrily. "Two days of hiding from you bastards in mud and sinkholes, caves and rotted logs."

"Not from me, honey," Fargo said. "You look as though you could stand something to eat." She didn't answer and he reached out, took her arm, and pulled her from the tree. "Come on," he said, and she followed grudgingly. She cast a wary eye on him as she walked beside him and he saw a small, upturned nose, mostly covered with dirt, a square face and strong jaw. She could be real cute under all that caked-on grime, he mused. "You've a name," he said.

She didn't answer for a moment. "Betsy," she said finally. "Betsy Cobb."

"All right, now, Betsy," he said as he reached the little glen and the Ovaro. "Start telling me what this is all about."

She shot a sideways glance at him. "You're really not one of them?" she asked.

"I'm not one of anybody," Fargo said. "Now, I'll get you some beef jerky and we can sit down and talk."

"Talk about what I know about Uncle Zeb?" she asked as she slid to the ground near a birch.

"Whatever you want to tell me." Fargo fished the jerky from his saddlebag.

"Why not?" She shrugged, suddenly agreeable as she sat on the ground and looked up at him.

He turned, squatted down in front of her, and began to take the jerky out of its oilskin wrapper. He was using both hands to unwrap the food when, out of the corner of his eye, he saw her arm come up from behind in a short, sharp arc. He tried to twist away from the rock in her hand, but it crashed against his temple and bursts of red and yellow light exploded inside his head. He felt himself falling, shook his head, and glimpsed her standing, watching, and then the curtain of grayness came over him, smothering the flashing bright lights.

He didn't know how long he'd lain unconscious, but he was alone when he woke. He grimaced at the sharp pain in his temple. He sat up, let his eyes focus and the Ovaro came into view. The long rifle holster was empty, he saw, and he cursed softly. The beef jerky was gone, too, he noted as he pushed himself to his feet. "Little bitch," he muttered aloud. It was too dark to pick up her trail, but there wasn't a lot left of the night. He shook his head, cleared away the last fuzziness in it, and pulled his bedroll into the thick brush. He lay down and drew a deep breath as the anger simmered inside him. But he lay silent as a log as he listened to the night sounds. She had fled and only the humming of night insects came to his ears. He let himself catnap as the rest of the night slowly moved toward dawn.

He was in the saddle when the new day came, and he picked up her trail easily enough. She'd gone west after she'd slammed the rock into his temple, half-running for a spell, he noted, then finally slowing. The morning sun took to the skies and Fargo saw her footprints wander north, then east, then turn west again. She had moved aimlessly, he saw, and he halted where the grass was tamped down in a small flat circle. She'd stopped there to rest but gone on again. Now her prints were in a straight line and he saw her footsteps had begun to drag across the ground. She was exhausted, and the dawn had come over her by the time she'd reached here. He reined up, slid to the ground, and began to follow on foot.

A flash of blue in the distance caught his eyes, morning sun glistening on a lake, but her trail turned right and he spied the small cave only a dozen yards ahead, well surrounded by thick brush. She had his big Sharps, he reminded himself as he dropped to his stomach and began to crawl forward. She was scared, angry, and vengeful, and she wouldn't hesitate to use it.

The mouth of the cave was small and low, and he paused a dozen feet from it. A line of small, loose pebbles ran across the entranceway and Fargo cursed inwardly. There was no way to cross over them into the cave without dislodging at least a half-dozen. She'd snap awake and he'd be framed in the entranceway, a perfect target for the big Sharps.

His lips drew back and he crawled sideways to the left side of the cave, where a growth of scrub brush afforded ample cover. He slid behind the brush and settled down. She'd sleep through the morning, he guessed, and he relaxed against the rock outside the cave. The sun had just crossed the noon sky when he heard her, and he rose on one knee, his gaze on the mouth of the cave. She crawled out, the rifle in one hand, stood up, and looked out across the forest land. She held the rifle casually in one hand as she stepped forward, obviously convinced she'd gotten away safely.

Your second mistake, honey, Fargo murmured silently as he waited a moment longer. She was still caked with dirt and grime, he noted, with a few new layers added. He rose up on the balls of his feet and let her take another few steps forward.

Her back was to him as he catapulted out of the scrub brush. She heard him and tried to turn, but he was on her as she attempted to bring the rifle up. He twisted the gun from her hands and she let out a half-cry, half-curse of pain. Stumbling backward, she tried to kick out and dive for the rifle where it landed on the ground. He stuck his foot out and she tripped, sprawled on the ground, and he was at her in one long stride. Reaching down, he picked her up by the rear of her belt and shirt, lifted her clear of the ground, and carried her to the Ovaro. He flung her facedown across the saddle and heard her gasp of breath. Scooping up the rifle, he swung onto the horse behind her and set the pinto into a gallop. She bounced up and down on her stomach, her little rear rising and falling, and he heard her grunts of pain.

"Damn you," she managed to gasp out. "Stop. I can't breathe."

"Take little breaths," he said as he kept the pinto at a gallop.

"Bastard," she managed between bounces.

The sparkling blue of a lake rose up in front of him; he headed the horse toward the water and saw a small, U-shaped lake where narrow-leafed sandbar willows grew to the very edge along with high and thick marsh grass. He rode to the edge of the water, let the pinto go in up to his elbows, and halted. Reaching one arm under her legs, he lifted and flipped the girl off the horse, backing the pinto away as she hit the water with a loud splash. He continued backing until the horse was on the soft sand at the edge of the lake.

In the water, Betsy sank, surfaced, flailed her arms, and he saw the mud and grime washing from her.

"Get it all off," he yelled, and she tossed him a glare as she dived again, went underwater, and came up shaking her head, this time with her face clean and her short blond hair free of matted leaves. He'd guessed right. She was indeed cute, with a small pug nose, the hint of freckles, and flashing blue eyes that still glared at him. She treaded water as she called to him.

"I knew you were one of them, you bastard," she said.

"You were wrong before. You're still wrong," he said.

"Hell I am," she said, and turned in the water and struck out across the lake, her arms moving with short, vigorous strokes.

He stayed in place and watched her swim and saw she started to move toward the shore when she was halfway across the small lake. He climbed onto the Ovaro, trotted around the edge of the water, and was waiting on the bank as she neared it. She halted, a dozen yards out, dived, and came up swimming hard in the opposite direction. Her watery path took her across the narrower part of the lake, and he waited, watched, and when she drew close to the shore, he sent the Ovaro around the lake and once again waited by the bank as she neared it.

She stopped, treaded water, and he saw the tiredness in her face, but she turned again and struck out along the length of the lake. Her strokes were slow now, but she maintained a steady movement; when she started to edge close to the shoreline, he sent the Ovaro forward again. He was waiting in front of her as she rose in the water, her arms hanging. She walked forward, stumbled, fell, lay half in the water for a moment, and rose again. With weary steps, she clambered out onto the bank and sank down to her knees.

"Had enough swimming?" Fargo inquired.

She glared at him, tiredness in her face. The wet clothes clung to her as a wet leaf clings to a log, outlining full, high, very round breasts where tiny points pushed into the fabric. The bottom of her shirt pressed against a short waist and the soaked Levi's were tight against full thighs that curved smoothly to her knees. She had a tight, curvaceous little body that somehow seemed to fit the pert pugnaciousness of her face.

"Bastard," she managed to get out between deep drafts of breath.

"You are a hard-nosed little package," Fargo said, not entirely without admiration.

She glowered at him as she still fought for breath and the very round high breasts pushed the shirt smooth. "Why'd you come chasing all the way up here after me if you're not one of them?" she accused.

"Two reasons," Fargo answered. "One, to get my

17

Sharps back, and two, to fan your little ass for clouting me with that rock."

She pushed herself to her feet and started to back into the water again. "You've got your damn rifle. You'll have to swim for the other," she said.

"Simmer down, dammit," Fargo said. "You're not as hard as you make out." She frowned in instant protest. "You had the chance to blow my head off after you clobbered me with the rock. You didn't take it. I figure we're even."

"How's that?" she snapped.

"I could've put a bullet into you a half-dozen times just now if I'd a mind to," he said, and she glowered as his words speared at her. "Whoever you've been running from, I'm not one of them," he said.

"Who are you?" she asked, suspicion still hard in her voice.

"Name's Fargo, Skye Fargo. Some call me the Trailsman," he answered.

"Trailsman," she grunted. "That's why you found me so easy."

"You owe me some answers for all my trouble," Fargo said.

Her pert face regarded him with a long glance. "I'll give you answers if you promise to help me," she said.

"You get only one promise, honey," Fargo growled.

"What's that?"

"I'll listen," he said.

She frowned as she considered his reply, let her lips tighten in displeasure. "Can I get out of these wet clothes first?" she asked.

"My pleasure, honey," Fargo said.

She half-turned and walked behind a thicket of giant bur reeds that almost hid her from view. He glimpsed flashes of her as she peeled off clothes and laid the shirt and the Levi's over the tops of the reeds where the sun could dry them. A pair of pink bloomers followed and he heard her voice as she settled down behind the giant reeds. "You listening?" she asked belligerently.

"I like to see a person's eyes when I talk to them," Fargo said. He waited and her head appeared over the tops of the thicket of reeds and he could see broad, beautifully rounded shoulders. "Talk."

# 2

"It's all because of Uncle Zeb. They killed him and they're trying to kill me."

"Who?" Fargo asked.

She shrugged, almost defensively. "I don't know," she said.

"That doesn't help much."

"Hired gunslingers, maybe. But they killed Uncle Zeb, gunned him down two nights ago on the street right in front of the Bar and Bed," she said.

"That's the town pleasuring place, I take it," Fargo said.

"Yes, in Buffalo Corners. I was walking with him when these four gunslingers came out of nowhere and started shooting. Uncle Zeb wasn't carrying a gun, but it wouldn't have made any difference if he were. He didn't have a chance," Betsy said.

"How'd you get away?" Fargo questioned.

"I dived under a big Owensboro ice wagon, rolled out the other side, and ran down an alleyway."

"They didn't chase after you?" Fargo frowned.

"Not then," Betsy said. "I ran all the way home. Uncle Zeb and I lived in a small house just north of town."

"They came there looking for you?"

"Yes. Lucky for me, I saw them riding up. I went out a side window and ran. I didn't even have time to take my horse, but maybe that turned out to be good. They'd have probably caught me if I'd been on horseback. On foot, I could hide in all kinds of places. They tried to hunt me down for two nights and two days," Betsy said.

"Why'd they come after you so hard?" Fargo asked.

She shrugged again. "I don't know. Maybe because they're afraid I saw their faces. But I didn't. It was dark. I couldn't identify any of them," she said.

Fargo made no reply, but he silently discarded the explanation. Gunslingers didn't worry about things like that. "Whatever their reasons, they didn't find you, and I'd say you were lucky for that," he told her.

"I need more than luck. I need help."

"What do you figure I can do?"

"Go back to town with me. Maybe put the fear of God into whoever they are so they'll leave me alone," she said. "Or do to them what they did to Uncle Zeb."

Fargo's eyes narrowed as he thought aloud. "I like reasons when I start shooting. You've given me only words. You say your uncle was murdered in the middle of town, but you're short on who or why."

"I told you, I don't know. Just go back with me. Maybe we'll find out," Betsy pleaded.

"Go back with you and take on four gunslingers. You don't ask much, do you?" Fargo slid at her.

He saw the smoothly rounded broad shoulders lift

as she shrugged. "You don't look the kind who'd be afraid," she said.

"I'm not the kind who'd be stupid, either," Fargo growled. "I'll think some on this."

He turned from her and strode away, folded himself down on a mossy bank, and turned her story in his mind. It was still hard to believe that four gunslingers would be chasing her on the chance she'd recognize one of them. Maybe she was holding back a lot more than she'd told him.

He lay back and stretched his long, powerful frame. It didn't much matter if she were holding back or not. He hadn't the time or the inclination to get involved. The rustle of the giant bur reeds cut into his thoughts and he saw her hands pulling clothes from the top of the thicket.

His eyes were on the reeds as she came out from behind them a few minutes later, dressed and dry. Her hair was really on the dark side of blond, he noted, and she wasn't very tall, her figure compact and firm, a kind of vibrancy in her body. The high, very round breasts bounced in unison as she strode toward him on short, energetic steps. She came to a halt in front of him, hands on hips. "Well, are you going to help me?"

He raised an eyebrow at her. "You always make asking sound like a demand?" he returned.

She frowned. "I guess I don't like asking anything of anyone, and I always expect the worst answer."

"You're half right this time," Fargo said. "I'm hired to take six wagons north. I've a spare day before I'm to meet with them. I'll give you that day."

"I suppose it's better than nothing," she muttered. "You're all charm, aren't you?"

"What do we do first?" she asked, ignoring his comment.

"Go get your horse at the house," Fargo said.

"No, I don't want to go there now. Let's go to town first. I can ride with you," Betsy said.

"We get your horse," Fargo said firmly, and climbed onto the Ovaro.

Betsy made a sour face as he helped her into the saddle in front of him. The sides of her breasts were firmly soft as they pressed against his arms when he reached around her to hold the reins.

"You said they weren't after money. They had to have a reason to just gun a man down. Tell me about Uncle Zeb. Give me his whole name," he said as he sent the Ovaro into a slow trot.

"Zeb Wills," she said. "And there's nothing much to tell. He's been a bookkeeper most all his life, just a plain, old bookkeeper. I went to live with him when my ma died four years ago. I kept house and helped him with his paperwork. That's why none of this makes any dammed sense."

"You thinking that maybe somebody made a mistake?"

"It happens, doesn't it?" she said.

"It does," he conceded. "Your Uncle Zeb an average-looking man?"

"No," she said. "He was small and thin and a little stooped."

"No mistake, then," Fargo grunted.

The Ovaro moved down a long slope and the road came into view.

"The house is around the next bend," Betsy said, and Fargo spurred the pinto forward, took the long bend in the road at a fast trot, and enjoyed the

23

softness of Betsy's round little rear as it bounced against his groin.

The house came into view—a modest, frame structure—and he immediately saw the bay mare tied outside at the rear, a buckboard nearby. He rode up to the house, reined to a halt, and the door flew open. Fargo's hand flicked to his side and the big Colt was up and ready to fire instantly as a man came from the cabin. Fargo took in a big frame that carried a sagging beer belly, a florid face with stringy, balding hair.

"Damn, Zelda, it's Betsy," the man called out over his shoulder. "I told you somebody would bring her back."

The woman stepped from the house, damn near six feet tall, with huge breasts and the shoulders of a small ox.

"Thank God," the woman said, and Fargo took in a coarse face with black hair pulled back severely, lips that were a thin, hard line.

He looked at Betsy as she turned to stare back at him and he saw the panic in her eyes.

"Run. Get away from here," she hissed.

"It's all right, Betsy, you just come down now. Uncle Zeb will take care of you," the man said soothingly as he stepped forward.

Betsy stared at Fargo and he saw the wild panic stay in her face. "He's not Uncle Zeb. Get me out of here," she half-shouted.

The man halted, a chiding smile on his face. "And I suppose this isn't your Aunt Zelda," he said as the woman followed him. "No more games now, Betsy. No more games."

Betsy screamed her answer at Fargo. "Dammit, I

24

don't have an Aunt Zelda and he's not my Uncle Zeb," she said.

The man's eyes went to Fargo. "Can we talk some, stranger? We're much obliged to you for bringing her back."

"I think a little talking is in order," Fargo said as he swung from the saddle.

"No, goddammit," Betsy said, and tried to seize the reins. He caught her wrists and pulled her to the ground. "Damn you," she spit, and tried to kick at him.

He stepped back as he let her wrist go and she started to race around the back of the pinto. The big woman met her, seized her with both arms, and held her with ease. Betsy's struggles were wasted motion in her grip.

"Betsy's been a problem child all her life, mister," the man said. "She not only runs away all the time, she makes up these wild stories, tells them to anyone who'll listen." He tapped his temple with one finger, his eyes narrowed meaningfully. "She's not all there, mister. Damn shame, too, her being so pretty."

"Don't listen to him, dammit," Betsy screamed. "He's lying. He's not my Uncle Zeb. He's one of them. They both are." She fought, trying to break away from the big woman's grip, but had no more success than a fly in a black widow's web.

Fargo let his gaze slowly take in the beer-bellied man as Betsy continued to scream protests.

"I know what you're thinking, mister," the man said. "You don't know who to believe. She does put on a good story."

"The name's Fargo, and I'm thinking I want more than words," Fargo said, and cast another glance across at Betsy. "She told me her Uncle Zeb was a small, thin man." He surveyed the heavyset figure again. "Let's see you put on some clothes from inside the house."

The man's eyes narrowed for a moment, but he smiled understandingly. "Why, sure, Fargo. I'll bring some right out for you," he said, and disappeared into the house.

Fargo waited, met Betsy's eyes, and saw the terrible pleading in them. The huge woman holding her stared expressionlessly at him.

"Don't listen to him. He's making it all up," Betsy said.

Fargo pulled his eyes from her as the man emerged from the house with two shirts, a buckskin jacket, and a pair of trousers over one arm. As Fargo watched, he took off the shirt he wore and put on one of the others. It fitted perfectly, Fargo saw, and he watched the man change into the second shirt and the garments fitted the heavy figure without the slightest trouble. The man held up the trousers and Fargo saw that the cut of them would fit the man's heavy rump. "Got more clothes inside if you want to look at them," the man said.

"No need for any more," Fargo said, and felt the sadness curl inside him. No small, thin man's clothes would fit the beer-bellied figure.

"Oh, God, oh, God," he heard Betsy wail as he turned away.

"All right, Betsy, we'll go inside, now," the woman said, and picked her up as though she were a screaming six-year-old.

"No, don't listen to them. No, damn you, Fargo, no," Betsy screamed, her voice growing muffled as the woman carried her into the house.

"You're not the first one she's fooled," the man

said. "But she's our problem. We'll have to live with it."

"I expect so," Fargo murmured, and started to turn to the Ovaro, paused, and glanced at the big hand the man held out to him.

"We're really obliged to you," the man said.

Fargo nodded, clasped the extended hand quickly, and swung onto the Ovaro. He felt the sourness inside him and realized he disliked turning his back on Betsy Cobb. But the man had provided the proof he'd asked for and he remembered how she had balked at coming to get her horse. Probably because she'd been afraid someone might be home. Damn pug-nosed little package, Fargo swore silently. Her feistiness had gotten to him more than he'd realized: she had certainly fooled him with her story. She'd had every piece of it down smooth as silk; how she'd fled the shooting, then how she'd run on foot the second time, and all the places she'd hidden. But then he'd always heard that the insane could sometimes make themselves seem sound as a gold piece. And she'd never come up with any reason for her uncle to be gunned down.

Fargo slowed the horse at the bend in the road, cast a long glance back at the house, and swore at himself. He kept feeling as though he were running out on her, and he'd no damn reason to feel that way, he told himself angrily. Yet he couldn't shake the feeling that he'd missed something back there at the house. He shook his head angrily, sent the Ovaro on, and went over everything that had happened up to the proof the man had produced at his demand. He came up with nothing, and yet the damn dissatisfied feeling stayed inside him. It had to have been Betsy, he grunted. Her fury had seemed too damn

27

real to be nothing more than the concoction of a demented girl. Yet maybe fury could be faked just as thoroughly as wild, involved stories.

"The hell with it," Fargo rasped aloud as he sent the pinto into a fast canter. He needed a bourbon. He hadn't the time to get involved with anything, anyway, so it had turned out for the best. Maybe he was just bothered by the distasteful way it had come to an end, he told himself, and hurried the pinto onward.

He shook away further thoughts about Betsy Cobb and her Uncle Zeb and let his eyes sweep the terrain as he rode. The Nevada Territory mixed harsh, dry land with jagged, steep-sloped desert high land filled with tall cones and pinnacles of rock, and sudden low-lying lakes and green areas. The Spanish had named the land when it was part of Mexican territory and it had lain possessed mainly by the Indians and desert wood rats for uncounted years until the Comstock lode brought thousands of men as stupid as they were greedy.

They fought and mined and died, and only a pitiful few left with any silver. Those who ventured too far from their mines often had their last claim staked out by a Shoshoni arrow. The Bannock, and sometimes the Nez Percé strayed down from the north, but mostly this was the home of the Shoshoni, who were as wily as they were formidable. Most of all, they knew how to live off the harshness of the land, and the intruder's pain became their ally.

Fargo slowed the pinto as he saw the buildings of the town come into view just as dusk began to slide across the land. Buffalo Corners nestled in a dip of the land north of the end of the Big Smoky Valley and within sight of the Shoshoni Mountain range. It was not unlike most such towns, Fargo noted as he rode in, except that the smell of cattle and the sight of cattle pens were markedly absent. No cow town astride the cattle trails, Buffalo Corners was a dusty oasis for those who wanted to cease their wandering, if only for a night.

Fargo reined to a halt when he saw the sign that read BAR & BED over the doorway of a lighted building. At least Betsy hadn't made up that, too, he grunted grimly as he hitched the Ovaro to the post and stepped into the large room. A pall of cigar and cigarette smoke hung in the air and Fargo's glance swept the girls that dotted the room, some at the handful of tables, others against the walls. Even thicker smoke wouldn't help them, he muttered silently as he walked to the bar. He ordered the bourbon he'd promised himself, and the bartender, a stocky man with close-cropped gray hair and shrewd eyes, took his money and tried to give him a shot glass of bar bourbon.

Fargo took a sip and set the glass down. "You charged me for good bourbon," he said quietly. "That's what I expect, mister."

The man merely shrugged as he poured another glass from another bottle, this one properly smooth and rich.

Fargo downed it and ordered another as the sourness stayed inside him like something improperly digested. He saw the woman move along the bar toward him, ample figure encased in a too-tight green dress, hair hard yellow as a brass bedstand, powder and paint trying to hide the years. Not succeeding, he grunted.

" 'Evening, big man," she said. "I'm Lily. I run this place." Fargo nodded at her and ordered another bourbon. "Whiskey's only one of the things we have to offer around here," the woman said. "Especially to big, good-lookin' strangers."

Fargo half-smiled as his gaze circled the room. "No offense, Lily, but your fillies have all gone to the post too often for me."

The madam's eyes hardened at once. "Particular, are you? My customers like what I have for them," she said.

"They also let you pawn off rotten bourbon," Fargo said pleasantly. "Sorry, doll, not this customer."

"You're the kind that prefers a bottle, is that it?" the madam pressed.

Fargo's lips pursed as he thought for a moment. "Truth is, I could use losing myself with a warm woman tonight," he said reflectively. "It might help get rid of the taste inside me."

"My girls can do that for you," the madam persisted.

"I said warm, not worn out," Fargo answered mildly.

"Bastard," the madam hissed.

Fargo shrugged as he finished the bourbon. He'd expected the woman to stalk away, but she stayed and he caught her exchange of glances with the bartender. "You can get what you're looking for right next door, small house with a window box of begonias," the madam said, and Fargo turned a glance of surprise at her.

"You recommending the competition?" he said.

"She came here to work for me, but she wanted the kind of money my customers won't pay. I had to turn her down, but she's young and real beautiful," the woman said. "Name's Ida Mae. Go see her and tell her Lily sent you."

"So's you can get your cut?" Fargo smiled.

"No, I'm just doing her and you a favor. I'm sentimental," the madam said.

"As a cactus." Fargo smiled back. The woman's jaw snapped shut and he tossed a coin at the bartender and pushed from the bar. "I might just pay the lady a visit."

He strolled away, made his way outside, and paused to draw in a deep breath of the night air. He saw the small house with the window box of begonias, a dim light visible through a curtained window. The idea of losing himself with a warm woman still appealed. That and curiosity made him turn and stroll down to the house. He knocked softly and waited.

The door opened after a few moments and the girl looked out at him. He felt his eyes narrow as he took in a thin, waiflike face, straight brown hair, and pale, washed-out blue eyes, a figure that was narrow-shouldered under a gray dress that hung in a straight, shapeless line.

"Yes?" she asked tentatively.

"You Ida Mae?" he asked, and she nodded.

Fargo felt the wry smile curl inside him. He could almost hear the madam and her bartender laughing. The woman had taken this way to pay him back for insulting her shopworn girls. He didn't really care about that, but he suddenly felt sorry for the thin, waiflike creature waiting in front of him.

"I think there's been a mistake," he said.

Her round, brown eyes stared solemnly back. "Lily sent you, didn't she? From the Bar and Bed," she said.

Fargo drew a deep breath. "Yes, I'm afraid so," he admitted.

"What'd she tell you?" the girl asked.

"It's no matter, Ida Mae," Fargo said gently.

"It is to me," Ida Mae said firmly.

Fargo felt his lips tighten. "She said that you'd asked to work for her but that you wanted more money than her customers would pay."

Ida Mae's smile surprised him, a quiet sadness in it. "But you came anyway," she said.

Fargo grimaced again and felt uncomfortable. "She said you were what I was looking for. I insulted her girls. She also said you were young and real beautiful."

"I'm sure you must be real disappointed," Ida Mae said, and Fargo searched her thin face. He saw neither sarcasm nor bitterness in it, only a quiet sadness.

"How about surprised," he offered.

She smiled again in her sad way. "You're kind," she said.

He swore at himself. She was right. He was being kind, and kindness could hurt more than truth sometimes. "I'm sorry I bothered you, Ida Mae," he said. "I'll be going along now."

"Wait," she said. "Come in, please. I'd like to tell you what really happened."

"Why?" Fargo asked.

"I don't like to be thought a fool," she said. "I know I could never be one of Lily's girls. I wouldn't go over there for that." She opened the door wider, and he shrugged and stepped into the house to find himself in a neat living room, lace doilies on chairs, an old rug with the frayed edges neatly sewn together, a dressmaker's figurine in one corner. He returned his glance to Ida Mae.

"You saying you did go to the Bar and Bed?" he asked.

Ida Mae drew a deep sigh, and to his surprise he saw a hint of tiny points press against the fabric of the straight gray dress. "Yes, I did," Ida Mae said.

"But only to try to get some extra work cleaning or laundering or waiting tables. Lily told me any girl working for her also services her customers." Ida Mae paused and her pale eyes met his gaze as the wistful, tiny smile came to her thin face again. "And you know what? I even agreed to that. I amazed myself. I've never done anything like that before and I agreed, *I agreed*."

"Why?" Fargo questioned.

"Same reason I went there to get extra work. I need money real bad. I've a mother in Oklahoma who's taken sick. She needs someone with her all day and I've got to get the money to her for that. I make just enough to support myself by sewing and some dressmaking. I've nothing left over. I was desperate, simple as that."

"Lily turned you down," Fargo said.

"She laughed at me," Ida Mae said.

"Now what do you figure to do?" Fargo asked.

The narrow shoulders shrugged helplessly. "I don't know," she said. "I wouldn't make any better bank robber than a dance-hall girl, I guess.

"No, you wouldn't," Fargo said wryly. "By the way, I'm Fargo . . . Skye Fargo."

"Thanks for listening," she said. "But I've something else to say, Fargo."

"I'm still listening," he said.

"Maybe we shouldn't waste your being here," Ida Mae said.

Fargo's eyes narrowed. "You saying what I'm thinking?"

"You came over because you didn't want Lily's worn-out girls. I know I'm not what you expected, but I'll try my best. Call it amateur night, if you like, but I still need to get that money to my ma. If you're still feeling kind, I'd be willing to try," she said.

Fargo searched the pale-blue eyes and saw only the quiet desperation in them. "I tell you what, Ida Mae. I'll give you twice what any of Lily's girls would've asked. You just take the money and send it to your ma," Fargo said.

She blinked solemnly at him. "Why would you do that, Fargo?" she asked.

"I can always stand a few good deeds on the books. Helps to balance out things." He grinned.

"You're more than kind. You're a good man. But I couldn't do that, take money without doing anything," she said.

"Why not?" He frowned.

"Pride and principles, I guess," she said firmly.

He smiled at her. "You're willing to do something gals without principles do because of your principles. Doesn't make much sense."

"Not the way you put it, on the outside. But it does on the inside," she answered.

"All right, Ida Mae. I wouldn't want to tamper with your principles, crazy as they are. Let's get down to some enjoying," Fargo said, and watched her turn, lead him into a small, neat bedroom with a large bed covered with a single white sheet that seemed appropriately virginal. She had her own quiet pride and that very own set of principles. He'd not make it seem like a good deed. He'd call on a principle of his own—namely, that a dish is as good as its chef. She turned to him, her eyes wide. "I've one rule, Ida Mae. You've got to enjoy it," he said.

She looked frightened for a moment. "I don't know. I want to, but I don't know. There were boys, a few, when I was young, but I've never done this before, not like this," she said.

"Be quiet, Ida Mae," Fargo said. He put one arm around her and felt more substance than he'd expected under the shapeless gray dress. He pulled her to him, pressed his mouth to hers, and felt her stay passive, almost motionless. He held the kiss, pressed his tongue forward to touch her lips, and she gave a sudden shudder. But he felt her lips part, begin to respond, and her mouth came open, met his tongue as she returned his kiss with a combination of tentativeness and eagerness.

"Oh, oh, my," she breathed as his hand moved up her back through the fabric of the gray dress. He pushed her gently down to the edge of the bed and drew his mouth from hers. A faint flush had spread over the thin, waiflike face, and the pale eyes had taken on new depths. He undid his gun belt, let it slide to the floor, and swung his long legs up onto the bed and lay back.

"Take my clothes off, Ida Mae," he said. She looked at him, the pale eyes wide, and her tongue came out to wet lips suddenly gone dry. "Your own time, your own way, but you do it," he said.

She swallowed and slowly leaned forward, and he watched her hands come up to the neck of his shirt. She began to undo buttons carefully, almost methodically, until she had the shirt fully unbuttoned. He moved his body to slide the shirt off and saw her eyes move across the powerful, muscled beauty of his chest and shoulders. He took her hand, pressed the palm against his skin, and she gave a little gasp. He kept her hand there as he slid his boots off. Her eyes averted, she moved her hand across his chest, pressed the powerful pectoral muscles, let her hand

35

move down across his flat, hard abdomen, and he heard her breath grow harsher.

"The trousers now, Ida Mae," he said softly. She swallowed and her fingers began to unbuckle his belt, twist at the top buttons of his Levi's. She had arrived at the third button, her eyes staring at the Levi's as they came open, when he reached down and took her wrist. "The dress now," he said. "Take it off."

She stared at him and sat motionless, and he rose up on one elbow, found the hem of the shapeless garment, and lifted.

"Oh," she gasped as he brought the dress up, slowly at first and then in a quick, sharp motion that flung it over her head. Her arms folded across her breasts instantly as she sat naked in front of him and looked away from his gaze. Surprise poked at him again as he took in a slender figure with more flesh on it than he'd expected, a rear that curved nicely up into a very long waist. A flat belly held a perfectly round little dot in the center and, below it, a modest triangle on the thin side. He reached out, took both wrists in his hands, and slowly, gently drew her arms down.

Ida Mae gave a tiny, shuddered sigh, and he saw small breasts, on the flat side on top but with the cups gaining a little shape, enough to turn up with a sharp, piquant lift that ended in very pink, surprisingly long nipples. A most unusual body, he noted, that of an adolescent and a woman mixed in together, a little of one here and a little of the other there.

He let her wrists go and she didn't bring her arms back up to cover the small-peaked breasts. "Now go on, Ida Mae," he said. "Finish." Obediently, she began to undo the last of the buttons on his Levi's, her eyes fastened on him as each came undone. He lifted his rear and let her draw the Levi's off the powerful thighs, down past steellike calves until he lay with only the bottoms of his drawers still on.

He felt himself responding to the climate he had set up for her, and his maleness rose, pushed the garment up, sought to burst free. "Go on, Ida Mae," he said as she stared down at him, and he saw the tiny beads of perspiration that had suddenly formed over her slender, naked body.

"Oh," she gasped out, a tiny sound hardly audible. "Oh."

"Go on, Ida Mae," he said again. Her hands came up to the tops of his drawers as her eyes stayed fastened on the moving, bulging force that strained to come out. With a sudden, quick motion, she yanked the drawers down, pulled them from him.

"OH, Oh, God . . . aaiiiiieee," Ida Mae screamed as his maleness quivered upright, seeking, throbbing. She flung her body forward over him, pressed hard against his throbbing firmness as she clasped him around the hips and pressed her face into his belly. "My God, oh, my God, oh . . . oooooh," she cried out as she lay pressed over him, as though she were using her body to provide a shield of modesty.

He reached down, half-lifted, half-pulled her up to his face, and felt the modest triangle rub against his wanting organ. Ida Mae cried out again, "Oh, oh, . . . oh, my." He cupped one hand around a small breast and she gasped, stiffened, and went limp again. His thumb moved gently over the long pink tip and felt it grow firm almost at once. Ida Mae moaned, an unexpected, low, long breath, and he drew his hands slowly down the length of her slender, long-waisted body, lowered his lips to her skin, and let his tongue lick the tiny beads of perspiration, traced a path down across the flat abdomen under the small-peaked breasts.

"Aaaaah . . . oooooh, oh, my God," Ida Mae moaned, and as his lips came up to close around one tiny peaked tip, the moan became a sharp scream. "Aiiieee . . . oh, God, oh, no, no," she cried out, and the long, slender body began to twist and writhe.

Her hips lifted, turned to one side, then the other as he caressed the tiny breast with his lips, pulled gently on the long very pink tip, and felt her hands dig into his shoulders. He drew his mouth away and she dug her hands harder into him. "No, no, don't stop, oh, don't stop," Ida Mae half-screamed, and grew silent as he drew her into his lips again. Her hands lifted, moved up along the back of his neck into his hair as she moaned again, her body twisting toward him.

He lowered his hand, pressed firmly into her flat belly, moved down to the modest triangle. "Oh, no, oh, Fargo . . . oh, oh, oh, be careful, oh, God," Ida Mae screamed, each word gasped out as his fingers moved down to press in between the dampness of her thin thighs. She screamed again and held her legs tight together, and he paused, rested, let his fingers gently press deeper, inch their way between the damp thighs. "No, no," Ida Mae breathed as she kept her thighs tight.

"All right, Ida Mae," Fargo whispered, relaxed the soft pressure of his hand, started to slide his fingers back. Her quick scream matched the sudden twist of her hips as she flung her thin thighs apart, clutched at his arm, pulled his hand to her almost flat pubic mound. "Please, oh, please," Ida Mae screamed, and

38

the scream became a wailing sound as his hand entered the wetness of her, touched gently, caressed, and felt her tightness as she thrust her hips upward.

Her hands were against his buttocks, pushing, pulling, trying to bring him over atop her. Suddenly Ida Mae was a crying, demanding explosion of desire, unwilling to wait, unwilling to go slow, unwilling to do anything but satisfy the devouring hunger that had burst forth inside her. He felt her hands become little fists and beat against his buttocks and thighs, and he realized that she was suddenly like a six-year-old in the throes of a terrible tantrum, beyond listening, beyond reaching, beyond everything except what she had to have.

He turned, came over her, drew himself to the now open portals, and her thin legs rose up, hit against his sides. He pushed into her, discarding ideas of being gentle. Ida Mae didn't want gentle, not now. Her scream was made of pain and pleasure, protest and passion, the adolescent and the woman all wrapped together in the explosion of new sensations. But the wisdom of the flesh transcended all else, and Ida Mae began to pump with him, her long waist drawing in and out, her thin body not unlike a suddenly hot wire. Her screams were sounds she had never uttered before and would never utter in exactly the same way again, and when he felt her almost flat pelvis begin to quiver, her tightness grow even tighter around him, he let himself explode with her.

Ida Mae screamed, a long, quavering cry that hung in the air until she sank down on the bed as though everything inside her had shriveled up and blown away. Her hands fell to her sides and she lay beside him with tiny tremors coursing through her thin body that made the small-peaked breasts jiggle. Finally her hand reached out, touched his hard-muscled body. "I wanted to be so good for you, but everything just happened. I didn't know what I was doing, everything came so fast," she said.

"You were fine. Best amateur night a man could want," Fargo said reassuringly.

Ida Mae half-turned, rose on one elbow, and leaned against him, the long nipples flattening against his chest. "It was so wonderful for me, even though I can't really remember much. I was in some kind of other world," she said.

"Good," Fargo said. "It'll all come back to you. Sometimes it takes a while."

Her waiflike, wide-eyed face looked up at him with a kind of wonder and awe mixed together in it. "You made your rule happen, Fargo. I loved it, God, did I ever," she said.

"I'm glad," Fargo said.

She leaned half across his chest, the tiny peaks resting on his pectoral muscles. "I guess I showed Lily, though she's never going to know it," Ida Mae murmured.

Fargo cupped her face with one big hand. "You getting ideas, Ida Mae?" he asked.

The small, sad smile came to the waiflike face. "No, no ideas. I know better, Fargo. The others wouldn't be like you, not in any way. This was a special night, yours and mine. It'll stay that way for me."

"Good girl," Fargo said, and leaned over to kiss one small peak.

"Stay the night, Fargo," Ida Mae said.

"I was planning on it. I've another rule," he said,

and her eyes waited. "Once is never enough for special moments," he said.

Ida Mae's thin face broke into an excited smile. Her arms flew around him and she half-climbed atop him. "Never, never enough," she echoed, and pressed her mouth to his as her thin body wriggled with adolescent enthusiasm and womanly wanting. His arms circled her and held her tight, and she was on fire almost at once.

Ida Mae was her own kind of special woman, he reflected as he began to make love to her again.

# 3

Morning brought a hot sun with the new day, and Fargo swore softly to himself as he sent the Ovaro over a low rise. The damn feeling was still inside him, the strange dissatisfaction that kept jabbing at him. He'd expected it would be gone, finished, and forgotten after the night with Ida Mae. She'd been a welcome surprise in every way, an unattractive body made enchanting by her fresh, unspoiled warmth and wanting. She had been preparing to send the money to her ma when he'd left and paused only to cling to him for a long moment. It had been more than just good with Ida Mae. It had been fun and somehow rewarding. But the damn sourness was still with him.

He rode on high land that took him near enough to the ridge to let him glimpse the small frame house below as he rode past. He saw the man outside and watched him split a length of log with one blow of his ax.

Fargo spurred the Ovaro on and pushed away the

feeling that continued to jab at him. He had other things to tend to, other commitments to keep, he told himself angrily as he sent the Ovaro down a long slope. He headed for a place beside a tributary of the Humboldt that had been given the name of Fools Point. It had become a starting point for wagon trains going north or west into the uncharted, wild land.

The letter that had hired him had included agreement money, the size of the wagon train, and the location of their meeting place, and was signed in a stiff hand by one Will Temple. Otherwise, it had said nothing about destination except that they wanted to reach a place on the other side of the Shoshoni Mountains. But he was used to that. Most wagon trains had only a general idea of where they wanted to go, and he sent the pinto up along a high line of dwarf maple, rode hard, and finally moved down through open ground covered with chickweed. He saw Fools Point come into view, three wagons standing close to one another: two big Conestogas, the third a high-sided Texas cotton-bed wagon outfitted with top bows and heavy canvas.

As he rode to a halt, a figure emerged from the rear of the first Conestoga near the edge of the shallow river. Fargo saw a slight-built man with a round face utterly devoid of any strength, bareheaded and revealing thinning hair. The man swung to the ground and approached him, and as Fargo dismounted, he saw the woman step from the wagon. She came up to stand beside the man, taking her place with a prim quietness, her plain, somewhat pinched face with no more strength in it than his.

"You're Fargo," the man said, and his smile was

earnest. "I was told you rode a fine Ovaro. I'm Will Temple."

"My pleasure," Fargo said.

"My wife, Amy," Will Temple introduced, and the woman seemed almost about to curtsy.

Fargo's glance went to the Conestoga as the figure stepped from behind it, a young woman carrying a bucket of water. Tall, wearing a brown, high-necked dress, she sat the bucket down and regarded him with brown eyes that held cool, quick appraisal. She had a straight nose, well-shaped lips that were fuller than she allowed them to be, a nice, clean-lined chin, a graceful neck, and thick deep brown hair she held pulled back severely into a bun. Wide shoulders held very straight pulled her modest breasts high, thrust forward with nicely curved cups. The dress outlined a long, narrow waist and concealed the rest of her figure with loose folds.

"My daughter, Ruth," Will Temple said, and Fargo nodded at the young woman. She acknowledged the nod with a flick of her eyes as she continued her cool appraisal of him, and he saw her take in the chiseled strength of his face, her gaze lingering on the breadth of his shoulders.

"Glad you're here, Fargo," Will Temple said, and Fargo brought his eyes to the man. "I'm just working on a list of a few more supplies we have to take on."

"The list is finished. I did it this morning," Ruth Temple broke in crisply.

Fargo saw her father half-shrug, offer a little smile of gratefulness. "I thought we'd wait another day or two to go to Buffalo Corners and pick up the extra supplies," the man said to Fargo.

"That'd be wasting time. We can pick them up at

any trading post," Ruth said, and Fargo saw she made no effort to disguise the authority in her voice.

"I suppose so," the man said meekly. "But we'll still be held up a day or two. One of the horses came down with foreleg trouble."

"A cramp in the right tendon. I took him to a smithy in Buffalo Corners. He ought to be fine by tomorrow." Ruth again.

Will Temple shrugged, the gesture a small abdication. His wife nodded along with him.

"Guess we ought to introduce Fargo to the others," the man said.

"I'll do that right now," Ruth answered, and beckoned to Fargo with an authoritative nod as she started to move toward the nearest wagon. "We're all family," she said to Fargo. "Cousins, nephews, distant kin."

Four figures stepped from the Conestoga as he halted beside Ruth Temple, a middle-aged man with a stolid face and short-cropped graying hair, a woman with twenty pounds too much on a short figure, and two young boys, ten and twelve, Fargo guessed.

"Thomas Temple and Hilda," Ruth introduced. "The boys are Tom Junior and Denny."

"Welcome, Fargo," the man said, and the Trailsman thought he detected an edge of relief in his voice.

"I'm cooking tonight, stewed rabbit," the woman announced pridefully. "You'll take supper with us, I hope."

"I'd be obliged," Fargo said, and she beamed. Being a good cook and homemaker was a thing of happy pride with Hilda Temple, he saw, and he turned his eyes to the converted Texas cotton-bed wagon as the family stepped outside. A tall, thin man helped a not-unattractive woman from the wagon, his long face edging gauntness.

"Ham Saunders," the man said. "My missus, Eloise." The woman, direct brown eyes in what once was undoubtedly a very pretty face, smiled and was unable to hide the weariness in the smile. The canvas of the wagon pulled back and another figure swung to the ground, a young girl in tight Levi's and an equally tight shirt that clung to young, firm breasts. Fargo took in brown hair loose around a smooth, even-featured face, hazel eyes, and a short nose. A lower lip fuller than the upper gave her a slightly pouty expression. The girl regarded him with a long glance and he smiled inwardly. She worked hard at trying to be sultry, he took note. "Cousin Charlotte," Ham Saunders said.

"You can get to know everyone better at supper," Ruth broke in, and stepped in front of Cousin Charlotte. "There are other things I want to go over with you now," she said, and started back toward the first Conestoga. Fargo followed, caught up to her in two long-legged strides.

"From his letter, I thought your pa would be in charge," Fargo slid at her as they walked.

"He is," the young woman said.

Fargo smiled. "Bullshit, Ruthie," he said softly. "You're making all the decisions around here." Her eyes narrowed at him. "I'm wondering why."

"If so, I don't think the reasons concern you, Fargo," Ruth Temple said icily.

"I take this wagon train out, everything about it concerns me, Ruthie," Fargo said.

"Ruth," she snapped.

"Whatever." He shrugged.

Her eyes surveyed him. "I suppose my making decisions would bother a man such as you," she said.

"What kind of a man is that?" Fargo asked mildly.

"Conceited, opinionated, used to having his own way, especially with women," she said with cool disapproval.

"So far so good." Fargo smiled cheerfully. "Go on."

"I'm sure many women find you attractive in a certain animal, sensual way. So I suppose your attitude is understandable," Ruth Temple said.

"You'll excuse me if I'm not real humble," Fargo said. "And I still want to know why you're calling all the shots."

"I've had to be in charge since I was a little girl," she snapped, and he caught a hint of resentment in her tone.

"Why?" he inquired.

"Decisions have always scared my father, and Mother's been a shadow of him," Ruth said.

"He decided to make this trip and I know many who wouldn't," Fargo commented.

"I decided for him," Ruth answered firmly.

"For him?" Fargo frowned.

"His job went out from under him. He was a finisher for a hat company back in Louisiana. Leaving, finding a new life somewhere else, was the only thing to do for him. But he sat on his hands with money running out until I made the decision for him," she said. "I sent the letter to you and Daddy signed it."

"No offense, honey, but what the hell do you know about where you're going?" Fargo asked.

"My older brother left home years ago and came

out here. He used to write and tell us what a wonderful place it was to start a new life," she said.

"When did you last hear from him?" Fargo asked.

"About a year back, but I wrote and told him we were coming," Ruth Temple said. "The kinfolk in the other wagons has their own reasons for pulling up stakes and they all decided to come along."

"That still leaves one thing, Ruthie," Fargo said.

"What's that?" She frowned.

"When those wagons start to roll, I'm in charge," he said.

Her smile was smooth. "I hired you because you're the very best," she said. It was a sideways answer, Fargo realized, but he decided to let it go.

"When do you expect the other three wagons?" he asked as they returned to the first Conestoga.

"There won't be any other wagons," Ruth said.

Fargo's brow furrowed as he turned to her. "The letter said there'd be six wagons," he protested.

"That was an error," she said loftily.

"You mean it was a lie," he growled.

"I mean nothing of the sort," she protested with more vigor than sincerity. "Besides, what difference does it make to you? You'll have three less wagons to concern yourself with."

"The difference is between being alive or dead," Fargo snapped. "You go through the Shoshoni Mountains, you need a force that can protect itself. Six wagons would be damn few to try it, but they'd have a chance. Three is suicide."

"You're exaggerating," she said.

"Hell I am. The Shoshoni will have you for breakfast," Fargo said.

"I hired you to see that that doesn't happen," Ruth threw back.

"I'm long on trailbreaking but short on miracles," Fargo returned. "Forget it."

"Absolutely not. I can't find another guide to break trail now. There's no time. Besides, I want you. You can't back out now. You agreed. You made a commitment. I thought you had a name for not breaking your word."

Fargo speared her with a long glance, his lake-blue eyes cold as ice cubes. She knew where to hit back, a combination of instinct and quick thinking, he conceded grudgingly. He had made a commitment, dammit, he swore. "All right, now I've got another one," he growled. "I've a commitment to keep you alive until you've sense enough to turn back."

She tossed him a quick, smug smile, but her voice held cool chiding. "I shouldn't expect that to happen if I were you," she said.

"Maybe I'm giving you credit for more sense than you have." Fargo shrugged and saw her brown eyes flare.

A figure stepped from the Conestoga and he saw Will Temple come toward him. "Ruth introduce you around?" the man smiled.

"She did, maybe to more than I wanted to know about," Fargo returned.

"Well, you'll have all our cooperation," the man said. "You can have my hand on that, Fargo."

Fargo looked at the hand Will Temple extended as he clasped it, almost a young boy's hand that had spent a lifetime working with felt and leather and showed it in its unmarked, smooth softness. As he stared at Will Temple's hand, he felt the frown suddenly dig into his brow, and inside himself thoughts were suddenly exploding like so many silent firecrackers. "Goddamn, that's it," he spit out as he dropped Will Temple's hand and saw Ruth stare at him.

"What are you talking about?" She frowned.

"Something that's been flying around inside me has just come to roost," Fargo bit out as he spun away and pulled himself onto the Ovaro. The hand burned in his mind—not Will Temple's but the one Betsy's Uncle Zeb had extended to him. No book-keeper's hand, not in a thousand years. It had been a hand of thick fingers with flat, stubby ends, scarred and gnarled, a hand that had spent a lifetime with hammers and axes, not pencils and pens, more ac-customed to logs than ledgers. The undefined sour-ness that had lain inside him had suddenly taken shape.

He heard Ruth's questions cut into his thoughts. "Where are you going?" she asked sharply.

"I might've made a mistake about something. I've got to be sure," he told her.

"You can't just ride off. When will you be back?" she yelled.

"Soon as I'm finished," he said, and sent the Ovaro into a gallop that sent a spray of dust into the air. He slowed as he crested the first ridge. It wouldn't help any to go barging back to the house without more proof. A bookkeeper could just possibly have done a lot of hard labor at one time and have a hand that carried the scars of many years back. It wasn't likely, but it was possible. Barging to the house with ques-tions wouldn't get him any new answers—not yet, anyway, Betsy would scream at him to believe her and the man would stand on the proof he'd already produced. Fargo, his lake-blue eyes narrowed, headed the pinto toward Buffalo Corners. He wanted to get some answers on his own before returning to Zeb Wills and Betsy.

Darkness was just settling down when he reached the town, rode to the saloon, and hitched the Ovaro to the rail. He saw a man closing the door to a barbershop a few yards up the street. "Hold on, friend," he called.

"Sorry, shop's closed for the day. Come back tomorrow morning," the man said.

"Need some answers, not a haircut," Fargo said, and the barber paused. "I heard there was a man gunned down a few nights ago right about here. You know anything about it?"

He saw the man's face grow tight at once. "No, not a thing."

"You hear anything about it?" Fargo asked.

"No, I wouldn't hear about that kind of thing," the man said.

"You must run a very unusual barbershop," Fargo commented as the man hurried away with a quick, nervous glance. Fargo watched him disappear as the sounds from the Bar & Bed drifted out to the street. He turned, pushed the saloon doors open, and went inside. A shooting right outside the saloon had to be heard inside, he reflected, and headed for the bar. He saw the madam cross the saloon to meet him as he reached the bar.

"Back again, big man?" she said. "Didn't you have yourself a good time with beautiful Ida Mae?" She followed the question with a burst of harsh laughter that the bartender echoed.

"Fact is, I did," Fargo said. "I stopped in to tell you how great she was." He watched the woman's hard face fall into an uncertain frown. "Got another

51

question while I'm here," Fargo said. "I was told a man was gunned down right outside your place the other night. You see it or hear it?"

The woman exchanged a quick glance with the bartender. "I don't know anything about any shooting."

Fargo glanced at the bartender and saw the man look away at once. "You see it or hear it?" he asked.

The man busied himself wiping the bar with a rag. "Not me," he said.

"You hear anybody talk about it?" Fargo pressed.

"Not me," the bartender said.

"You know a man named Zeb Wills?" Fargo questioned.

"Not me," the bartender said.

Fargo's smile was grim as he turned away and scanned the room. The evening was still early and only a few regular customers were on hand yet, along with Lily's tired girls. Fargo lifted his voice as he called out. "Anybody see a shooting right outside the other night?" he asked. The few men only returned silent stares. "Anybody hear it?" Fargo questioned, and got only more silence. He nodded, tossed a glance at the madam as she watched him with her hard face set tight. He strolled across the room and out of the saloon to halt outside.

No one had seen or heard anything, he murmured. Why? Because they were all frightened? Or because there really had been no shooting?

His lips pulled back in distaste. Maybe a book-keeper could have an old wrangler's hands. Maybe Betsy Cobb's story had been hollow, after all. He glanced down to the window box on the house a few yards away and suddenly felt the frown pull at him. Ida Mae would have heard a shooting. Her house was plenty near enough and she'd not play games with the truth.

She opened at his knock, her thin, waif's face staring at him until it broke into a squeal of delight. "Fargo," she said as she threw her arms around him. "I never thought you'd be back this soon."

"Neither did I," he said as he stepped into the house with her. "This is a different kind of visit, Ida Mae."

Disappointment flooded her face, but she quickly shrugged it away and leaned against him. "I'm still glad to see you," she said. "It'll help make my dreamin' that much better."

He patted her thin rear gently. "You're a good girl, Ida Mae. I was told there was a shooting a few nights ago right outside the Bar and Bed. You'd had to have heard it."

She frowned in thought. "A few nights back?" she echoed. "I didn't hear anything. But it could've been the night I was delivering an embroidered pillowcase to Jane Oates."

"Damn," Fargo spit out.

"But there was no one laying out on the street when I came back," Ida Mae said. "Of course, that doesn't mean anything much."

"Why not?" Fargo asked.

"Jay Bullock's pretty quick about buryin' folks," she said.

Fargo frowned as her words set his thoughts racing. "The town undertaker," he murmured, and she nodded. "Of course, dammit," Fargo snapped. "He'd know." He pulled Ida Mae to him and hugged her. "Thank you, honey. I've got to go visit the buryin' man."

"End of town, old shack, about a quarter-mile be-

53

fore the boot hill," Ida Mae said, kissed him quickly, and let him hurry away.

Outside, Fargo climbed onto the Ovaro and rode to where the old shack stood alone beyond the last of the town buildings. He saw a light in a window, and the door opened as he rode to a halt and swung to the ground. The man, in trousers and suspenders, looked at him from out of a long-jawed face that wore suspicion and caution.

"Somethin' you want, mister?" the undertaker questioned.

"Heard a man was gunned down in front of the Bar and Bed a few nights ago. You bury him?" Fargo asked.

Fargo saw the tension at once. "Who're you, mister?" the undertaker asked.

"Name's Fargo ... Skye Fargo," the Trailsman answered. "I didn't get your answer, friend."

The man's tongue came out to lick his suddenly dry lips. "Don't know about any shooting," he said.

"His name was Zeb Wills. You bury him?" Fargo prodded.

"Don't know any Zeb Wills." The undertaker swallowed nervously.

"You bury anybody the last few days?" Fargo pressed.

"No," the man snapped. His face had become a tight mask. "Clear out, mister. You're botherin' my sleep with all these damn-fool questions."

"Guess so," Fargo agreed quietly. "Sorry." He pulled himself back onto the Ovaro and turned the horse toward town as the man slammed the door shut. He kept riding to town until he was out of sight of the cabin and then swung sharp right and retraced steps in a wide circle. He ended up at the foot of the town's burying place, the boot hill common to almost every dusty, lawless town in the territories.

He slid from the horse and began to move slowly up the hillside on foot, carefully pausing at each mound of earth and at every token headstone made of a slab of wood or a piece of shale. He bent down under the pale moonlight to scrape first his foot and then his hand across each mound, making certain he missed none. He had reached the top of the hill before he dropped to one knee beside a small mound. His fingers dug into dirt that was still soft, dirt that the sun and wind hadn't had time to form into a hard crust yet. It hadn't been in place for more than a few days, he estimated. There were four other mounds across the top of the hill and he went to each just to be certain. They were all firm and dry, and he turned and hurried down to where he'd left the Ovaro.

He dug into the saddlebag and brought out a small spade he kept for digging up wild roots and tubers when the need arose. Climbing the hill again, he began to dig, the task painfully slow with the makeshift shovel. He didn't like digging graves and liked digging them up even less.

The moon had begun its descent across the night sky when he finally had the grave uncovered enough for him to see the plain pine box. He used the thick back edge of the spade to pry the cover loose; then he reached down, pulled the lid off, and stared at the figure in the box. He took in a small, slight-built, thin man, his chest caked with dried blood. He let his gaze go down to the man's hands where they lay stiff-fingered at his sides. Small, smooth hands, slender, unmarked fingers, a bookkeeper's hands. "Uncle Zeb," Fargo muttered aloud as he let the lid drop.

He began to push the dirt back into the grave, kicking it in with his boots first, finished with the little spade. He smoothed it down, and unless someone looked closely, it appeared pretty much the same as he'd found it. He got to his feet and walked down the hill to the Ovaro.

Betsy had been telling the truth all along, he realized. He'd been tricked into doing her an injustice, and he felt the anger of it simmer inside him. But there was more. Whoever had Zeb Wills gunned down had the power to put fear into others. His queries into the shooting had drawn only silence and evasions. Yet he still had neither the time nor the desire to get involved in whatever it was. But he'd do one thing: he'd get Betsy out of the hole he'd left her. He owed her that, and he owed himself. He wasn't proud of abandoning people that didn't deserve abandoning.

Dawn began to slide pink streaks across the sky as he rode east and he felt the weariness lying on him. He pulled the Ovaro under the low branches of a gambel oak, slid out of the saddle, and stretched his long, powerful frame on the soft bromegrass. He let himself sleep at once in the shade of the thick foliage overhead as the morning sun burned down. The morning had begun to nudge the noon hour when he woke, used his canteen to wash and wet his throat, and turned the Ovaro east again. He took the high land that brought him to where he could look down at the small house, and he reined up, the frown sliding across his brow. The door of the house hung open and the buckboard was gone. But he waited, peered down at the house, and when he was convinced it was deserted, he rode down to the rear of the structure where the buckboard had been.

The tracks were clear, not more than a few hours old, he saw, and he swung the Ovaro in behind them. They rolled west, into a gulley and up a long slope, stayed easy to follow as they rolled down into a red-clay arroyo. The buckboard had stayed in the arroyo until the desert valley came to an end and the tracks turned upward to where a small log cabin appeared, all but hidden away in a thicket of dwarf maple.

Fargo pulled up behind a series of jagged rocks at the side of the arroyo, slid from the Ovaro, and cast a glance at the sky. The sun had already begun to move behind the high rocks. Night would blanket the thicket of trees within the hour. He settled himself behind the rocks where a crevice let him see the cabin below.

The gray-purple haze of dusk finally began to settle over the land and Fargo saw the cabin door open. The big woman stepped out with a skillet, flung the scraps from the pan onto the ground, and disappeared back inside the cabin. But she left the door hanging ajar, Fargo saw, and as darkness pushed dusk away, he moved from behind the rocks. He dropped to his stomach and began to crawl toward the thicket, was nearing the cabin when he heard Betsy's voice in a sharp cry of mixed pain and anger. The sound of a hard slap followed, and Betsy's cry came again.

"Easy, now, Zelda," Fargo heard the man's voice call out. "We're supposed to keep her in shape for answerin' questions."

"I'm just going to enjoy her some," Fargo heard the woman say, and he inched forward again and drew the Colt from its holster as he reached the door. He pressed his eye to where the door hung ajar, and he managed a worm's-eye view of the cabin. A kerosene lamp had been lighted that threw enough light for the single room, and he saw Betsy, hands tied behind her back, lying atop a mattress on the floor. The huge woman stood over her.

"Bitch," Betsy mumbled. "Goddamn bitch." The woman yanked hard on her hair and Betsy cried out in pain.

"Now, you be nice, little girlie," the woman snarled.

Fargo heard the man laugh, shifted his eyes to the figure sitting on a straight-backed chair, a long-barrel Henry leaning against the wall a few feet from the chair.

"Careful, Zelda," the man said, cackling.

"That's it, girlie, that's it—nice, now," the woman cooed in a voice that sounded more like the scrape of nails.

Fargo pushed himself to his feet, yanked the door open, and stepped into the cabin. "Get away from her, you damn cow," he snapped, saw the woman freeze atop Betsy for an instant. Fargo barked again, and the woman moved from the mattress, her giant breasts swaying, her eyes dark with fury. Fargo threw a glance at the man. "Get up, away from the rifle," he said, and the man obeyed quickly for all his overweight girth. "Uncle Zeb, you're a goddamn liar," Fargo commented as he moved toward Betsy, and the man's face took on narrow-eyed cunning.

"You're making a real mistake, Fargo," the man said.

58

"Not this time," Fargo growled, and gestured with the Colt. The woman moved away from the mattress, but stayed facing him, eyes still filled with hate, the massive mounds thrusting forward.

Betsy's wide eyes welcomed Fargo with relief as he moved to the mattress, knelt on one knee, and used his left hand to start to untie her wrists. She turned her back too him so he could get at the bonds as he kept the Colt facing the man and the huge woman. The wrist bonds proved to be stubborn, and he took his eyes from the man for an instant to tear at the knot that resisted untying. His peripheral vision caught the flicker of movement and he swung his eyes to the man at once, saw he hadn't moved, and he swung his glance to the woman just as her arm hurtled forward. He saw the kerosene lamp coming through the air in an arc, directly at him, and he half-dropped, twisting away instinctively. The lamp grazed the back of his shoulders and smashed against the floor at one corner of the mattress to explode in a shower of flame. The old, tattered mattress caught fire instantly, old cotton and ticking blazing upward in leaping tongues of dancing flame.

Cursing, the Trailsman twisted away from the flames, ducked around the blast of heat, and raced across the mattress to Betsy as, hands still bound behind her, she tried to push herself to her feet. Dragging her with him with one hand around her waist, he glimpsed the woman through the dancing curtain of fire. The huge form raced for the rifle, and Fargo saw her reach it, scoop it from the wall, and spin. She fired two shots through the flame, but they slammed into the wall just to his right.

Still hanging on to Betsy with one arm, Fargo pulled her sideways with him as the woman got off another shot. He stepped beyond the edge of the flaming mattress and his finger tightened on the trigger. The Colt fired and he saw the bullet pierce through one huge breast. The woman staggered backward to the far wall and the rifle fell from her hands. A tongue of flame leapt toward Fargo and he pulled back, lifted Betsy from the floor with him as the searing blast of heat swirled close. He glimpsed the figure of the man streaking out of the cabin as he carried Betsy around the edge of the flaming mattress to the front of the room. The Colt ready to fire, he glanced at the woman, but she sat on the floor of the cabin, her back against the wall, unmoving. The bullet hole in the huge breast seemed ridiculously small, the tiny trickle of red unreal, but her massive form held the silence of the lifeless.

A blast of heat swept across the cabin and he whirled to see the far wall of the cabin burning furiously. Old, dry wood welcomed flame, and the rest of the cabin seemed to catch fire before his eyes with a wild glee. He lifted Betsy, slung her over his shoulder, and bolted for the door. As he raced outside, he flung himself to the ground with her, brought the Colt up to fire. But only the sound of the crackling flames behind him filled the night, and Fargo rose to one knee, took the double-edged throwing knife from its holster around his calf, and severed Betsy's wrist bonds.

"He's gone, running to save his neck," Fargo muttered as Betsy sat up and came against him.

"Thank God," she murmured. He felt the heat on his back as the entire cabin went up in flames, and he rose and pulled Betsy with him as he stepped away from the fire. Her eyes searched his face in the orange glow. "I didn't expect you'd be back," she said.

"I didn't either," he grunted.

"What did it?" she asked.

"Hands," he said, and Betsy frowned. "He didn't have the hands of a bookkkeeper," Fargo added, and she nodded slowly. "That and a few other things that didn't set right," he said.

"I found out why he had the clothes to fit himself," Betsy said. "They were sent to wait for me on the chance somebody would bring me back. They were ready with that story about my being crazy and the clothes to carry off his being Uncle Zeb."

"It almost worked," Fargo said soberly.

"Thank God for almost," Betsy said.

"You still have a horse back at the house?" Fargo asked, and she nodded. "Let's go get him," he said, and Betsy climbed onto the Ovaro with him, leaned back against him as he turned the horse northward. "Found out a few other things," Fargo said as they rode. "Whoever had your Uncle Zeb killed has a lot of clout around here, enough to give everyone a case of lockjaw. Got any ideas on who that might be?"

"Uncle Zeb worked for Ben Brookings. He's about the most powerful man around here," Betsy said. "But I can't figure why Ben Brookings would have his own bookkeeper gunned down."

"Not unless his bookkeeper knew too much or found out too much," Fargo ventured. "What's Ben Brookings do?"

"He owns the big haulage outfit that carries all the government-contract freight, grain, sugar, iron ore, borax, army supplies, sometimes gold and silver. Just about anything and everything."

Fargo's lips pursed as he thought aloud. "Sounds like he'd fit," he said. "But whoever it was thinks you know whatever Zeb knew."

"That means they'll be coming after me again," Betsy said with alarm. "Can you help me, Fargo? Stay with me."

"No, I've given my word to ride trail for a wagon train, such as it is," Fargo said, grimness coming into his voice. The house came into view and he hurried the Ovaro to a halt, slid to the ground with Betsy as her brown eyes searched his face.

"What do I do? Try to hide out again?" she asked.

"You can't stay here. They'll come looking here for sure, and you were lucky hiding out last time," he said, thinking aloud. "I guess you'd best come along with me."

She frowned through the hope that flooded her face. "Don't you have to ask about that first?" Betsy said.

"There are times to ask and times not to," he said. "Pack whatever clothes you'll be needing and get your horse."

She burst into a happy smile, wrapped arms around his waist, and hugged him to her and he felt the firm warmth of her chunky body. "I can't be thanking you enough," she said.

"Maybe you'll think of a way. Get moving," he said, and she took her embrace back and hurried into the house.

Fargo watched the moon rise into the sky and his thoughts went to the man that had fled the cabin. He could be trouble, Fargo knew, but he pushed away the thought. There was nothing to be gained by worrying trouble on. It'd come on its own quickly enough. He turned as Betsy reappeared with her saddlebag, hurried around the house to the rear, and returned with her horse. Fargo took the horse in with an expert's eyes, saw a brown mare with a white patch on her rump, a chunky, sturdy-legged horse that moved with quick energy. He smiled inwardly. They fitted, rider and horse, and he climbed onto the Ovaro and headed north once again.

"It's late," he told her. "We'll bed down and get to the others, come morning."

Betsy's glance was grateful. "I'm feeling real wrung out," she said. "It's been a long spell since I've had a good night's sleep."

"We'll try for it tonight," Fargo said as he pulled the horses into a half-circle where a small stand of serviceberry afforded a white-petaled refuge. He took care of the horses while she changed in the brush and emerged with a loose nightdress that revealed legs a trifle heavy but carrying the firm curving lines of youth.

Fargo undressed down to underdrawers and stretched out on his bedroll as Betsy lay down nearby on a blanket. She lay on her back, hands behind her head, and the very round, high breasts filled the top of the short nightgown, he saw.

"Why?" she murmured. "Why'd they kill Uncle Zeb? What's it all mean?"

"Could mean your Uncle Zeb came onto something," Fargo said. "Or maybe he was working his own deal. Whichever, somebody got onto it."

"It had to be Ben Brookings," Betsy said.

"Guessing games will only waste your time and energy," Fargo said.

"Maybe they'll just figure I don't know anything

and forget about me when I drop out of sight," Betsy said.

"It's important enough to somebody to kill for. They're not likely to forget about you. When I finish with this wagon train, we can come back and maybe nail it down," Fargo said. "Now get some sleep."

He turned on his side and listened to her settle into sleep. The night grew still and he let slumber sweep over him.

There'd be another kind of trouble, come morning, he was pretty damn certain.

# 4

The sun burned down bright and hot as he rode toward the three wagons with Betsy beside him. He let her sleep into the morning and she woke refreshed with bounce and energy, but he caught the apprehension that touched her pert face as they drew up to the wagons. "I talk, you listen. No sass from you, understand?" he said.

She frowned at him. "I don't like to go where I'm not wanted," she said.

"You'd like joining your Uncle Zeb better?" he snapped at her, and she turned away but her face stayed tight. He reined up and Ham Saunders paused in helping his wife shake out a quilt. Will Temple appeared from behind the big Conestoga and waved. Fargo swung from the horse and Betsy followed, stood close beside him as Ruth Temple stepped out of the Conestoga. She wore the same high-necked brown dress and her hair still pulled severely back into a bun. Her eyes held contained anger as she speared him with a long glance.

"How nice of you to stop by," she said, each word coated with acid, and her glance flicked to Betsy. "I take it you're not ready to move out," she remarked.

"You take it wrong," Fargo said. Ruth Temple glanced at him and returned her eyes to Betsy, icy questions in their brown orbs. "Betsy Cobb," Fargo introduced. "She's coming along."

Ruth Temple's icy calm shattered in surprise as she looked at Fargo. "What?" She frowned.

"She's coming along," Fargo repeated.

Ruth's frown deepened and her lips grew thin. "No she's not," she said slowly but very firmly.

"She's in trouble, and going with us is the only place for her now," Fargo said.

"What a convenient story," Ruth said. "You don't expect me to swallow that, do you?"

"I don't much care whether you do or don't, but she goes," Fargo said almost mildly.

"I didn't agree to you bringing anyone along, and certainly not your own private little trollop," Ruth snapped.

Fargo saw Betsy's face redden, her mouth open, but she caught his glance and pulled her lips closed. He turned his eyes back to Ruth. "I didn't agree to three wagons," he said quietly.

"That's not the same," she protested.

"It's a lot worse," Fargo said. "I'm not going to argue about it, Ruthie. She goes or I don't."

Ruth Temple's eyes burned into him. "This is blackmail," she hissed.

"No, it's what has to be done," Fargo corrected.

The others had gathered around, he saw, and it was Will Temple who spoke up. "If the girl's in trouble it'd only be Christian to help her," he said.

Ruth shot her father a glance of pure disdain.

"Typical," she bit out, spun on her heel, and climbed into the Conestoga.

Will Temple shrugged at Fargo and his hands fluttered aimlessly. "Ruth is very strong-willed, always has been," he said apologetically. He paused, his eyes holding on Fargo. "But I'd guess maybe you'll be able to hold your own with her," he said.

"I'll try," Fargo said blandly. "Get your wagons ready. We'll be pulling out."

"Ruth said there was a trading post about two miles north. We still have to lay in a few more supplies," Will Temple said.

"A few more than you know about," Fargo said, and turned the Ovaro away. "You ride with me," he said to Betsy, and she swung in beside him as he pulled up a dozen yards on and waited for the wagons to start. "You did real well," he complimented her with a grin.

Betsy's pugnacious face shot him a quick glower. "Don't expect it again," she snapped. "That tight-assed bitch calls me a trollop again, I'll flatten her."

"Wonderful," Fargo said. "You ever stop to think that might convince other folks that she was right? Or don't you ever stop to think?"

"I don't have to think. I feel," she snapped. "And I trust what I feel."

"Always?" Fargo asked.

"Always," she said firmly.

"Hard nose." He laughed and heard the creak of wagon wheels beginning to roll. He glanced back and saw Will Temple driving the lead wagon, Ruth sitting beside him. Tom Temple and his two boys were on the second Conestoga and Ham Saunders brought the Texas cotton-bed up in the rear.

Fargo turned the Ovaro north and set the horse

into a slow trot across gently rolling fields. Betsy rode beside him, the very round, high breasts bouncing nicely in unison. "I ought to tell you something while you've still time to bow out," he said. "I could be taking you from the frying pan into the fire."

"You mean the Shoshoni," she said, and he nodded grimly. "I figure I'm ahead for every day I'm alive," Betsy said. "And I think you're in more trouble than I am. You've Miss Stiff Back as well as the Shoshoni to worry about."

His glance narrowed at her. "You're meaning more than you're saying," he growled.

"She'd like to get you in the hay," Betsy said.

"Not her," Fargo disagreed. "She gets her kicks out of being in charge."

"That's another way of being in charge to her," Betsy said.

"You're letting your imagination run off with the bit, honey," Fargo said.

"I trust what I feel," Betsy said smugly, and he peered ahead to where the lone structure came into view against the horizon. He rode on to the trading post, dismounted, and waited for the wagons to roll up to a halt.

Ruth swung to the ground gracefully, he noted, and faced him with cool disapproval. "Father tells me you want some special supplies. What are they?" she queried.

"Four extra rifles for every person in these wagons," Fargo said.

"What in heavens for?" Ruth frowned.

"So's I can give you a chance to keep your scalp. Don't waste time with questions now. Just get the rifles and move out," he said brusquely.

Her lips drawing tight, Ruth spun, started into the

trading post, and beckoned to Ham Saunders to follow.

Fargo was back on the Ovaro when she came out carrying two rifles, Ham Saunders with the rest inside a wide canvas sling. Fargo waved an arm at the wagons and rode away, Betsy beside him. The rolling fields soon gave way to hard, red-clay dirt with knots of dwarf maple along the way, and the land began to rise into the foothills of the Shoshoni Mountain range.

He called a halt when the afternoon still had at least an hour of daylight left, and led the wagons to a place where a pyramid of rock protected one side and the dwarf maple bordered the other. He stayed in the saddle as the wagons settled into their places, and he saw Ruth stride toward him with icy disapproval in her face.

"I purchased the extra rifles, but it won't happen again that way," she said as she came to a halt. "From now on, I'll insist on three things: respectful answers to my questions, proper explanations to anything I ask, and your full attention to my opinions, in that order."

Fargo smiled back. "If there's time, if you deserve them, and if I feel like it, in that order," he said, and saw her lips tighten in fury. He wheeled the Ovaro around and called back to Will Temple. "I'm going to do some scouting. Be back for supper," he said, and sent the Ovaro north, stayed on the red-clay ground, and finally made a wide circle around the rear of the pyramid of rocks and rode south the way they had come. He took to the high, craggy land, slowed, and let the Ovaro pick his steps. He halted when he found a place that let him survey the land they had traversed, and his eyes slowly moved across the hills and hollows, rock formations and dry river-beds. The dusk came and took away the distant places. As darkness quickly followed, he turned the pinto and headed back north. He'd seen nothing to bother him, but only one full day had gone by. It was far from time to relax.

He saw the dim glow of campfire light as he neared the wagons and smelled the good smell of beans and stew. He was out of the saddle before the pinto came to a halt as he reached the campsite. Hilda Temple's ample figure hurried toward him with a tin plate piled high, her round face beaming. "Saved a plate for you, Fargo. It's real good tonight," she said.

"I'm sure it is. Much obliged, Hilda," he said, and drew another happy smile.

The woman hurried back to the fire and Fargo sat down alone and eagerly enjoyed the meal. Hilda Temple was a good cook, indeed, he commented silently. He saw Betsy sitting with Will and Amy Temple, and she waved at him as she cleaned her plate. The figure that came from the other side of the fire toward him walked with a slow, languid motion, and he finished the last of the meal as Cousin Charlotte halted, folded herself down beside him. He watched her hazel eyes scan him, the slightly pouty expression plainly her version of sultriness. It wasn't entirely a wasted effort, he decided. She radiated a simmering sensuousness, her tight Levi's encasing a rounded belly that curved into her hips in one smooth, unbroken line. She leaned back on her elbows, and her breasts curved upward with youthful firmness.

"Cousin Charlotte," Fargo murmured. "That mean you're Ham Saunders' girl?"

"No, I just live with Ham and Eloise. I'm a distant

cousin," she said, and nodded toward where Betsy was cleaning off her plate. "She what Ruth said?" the girl inquired. "Your private stock?"

"I wouldn't say that," Fargo answered.

Cousin Charlotte turned her hazel eyes on him, and he saw the unsaid dancing in their depths and her smile was made of private meanings. "You're not the one-woman kind," she said.

"And you're too young to know that," he returned.

"You know better than that," Charlotte said.

"I guess so." Fargo grinned. He considered probing further but decided against it as he saw Ruth Temple's tall figure marching toward him. She halted, her eyes on Charlotte.

"Hilda needs help cleaning up," she said, the remark an order.

Charlotte pushed to her feet, tossed a sly smile at Fargo as she strolled away. Fargo rose also, met Ruth's severe gaze. "You brought your own playmate. I'll expect you'll confine yourself to her," she said.

"That's not why I brought Betsy. I told you that," Fargo said. "Not that it'd make all that much difference."

"Meaning what?" Ruth frowned.

"A man can enjoy more than one kind of fruit. I like a good apple, a juicy orange, a sweet plum, a nice pear," he said. "Only one thing I don't much like."

"What's that?" she asked stiffly.

"Don't like prunes," Fargo said, and saw her lips tighten. He smiled pleasantly at her as she fought to keep her temper in hand. She succeeded and her eyes narrowed as she slid the question at him.

"What makes a man go scouting where he's been

instead of where he's going?" she asked, the edge of smugness in her voice.

His brows lifted in surprise and he allowed a slow smile. "You're real bright-eyed, aren't you?" he commented.

"I happened to take a walk and saw you coming back," she said.

"Try again," Fargo said. "You had to be up high on rock."

"Maybe. I like to look around. Anyway, I saw you," she said. "You were scouting behind us."

Fargo put words together in his mind before answering. She was suspicious, intuitive, and smart. She wouldn't be turned away with glib replies. "The Shoshoni will pick up a trail, swing around behind, and follow," he said. "It's a little early for that, but I like to be sure." He waited nonchalantly, saw her consider his answer and accept it.

"I like to be sure, too," she said tartly.

"A suspicious nature is bad for you." Fargo smiled. "It shrivels the spirit."

"My spirit is fine," she snapped. "Good night."

He shrugged. She stalked away and he watched her go, a tall, willowy figure held in stiffly. The fire had begun to burn down to embers and he saw Betsy approach as he took down his bedroll.

"I might as well stop by. Everybody else has," she said with a trace of waspishness. "Where are you going to sleep?"

"Up in the high rocks," he said.

She said nothing and her pert face grew soft. "Will Temple has been very nice to me. His wife, too," she said. "Miss Stiff Back makes like I'm not even here."

"She'll come around. Get some sleep. I'll pick up the pace tomorrow." Betsy nodded and walked away, and he took his bedroll and began to climb up the pyramid of rock. He finally found a place he liked, the surrounding rocks low enough to let him scan the entire area if he stood, and high enough to hide him as he slept. He undressed, put his gun belt at his side, and enjoyed the warm night breezes. He was almost asleep when he heard the sound, footsteps sending tiny pebbles of rock rolling down the passageway below.

A Shoshoni would be a damn sight quieter, he knew, but he drew the big Colt from the holster at his side and leveled it at the top of the passageway.

The short, blond hair appeared first, then the chunky figure pushing its way on hands and knees, and he lowered the Colt. "Damn, what are you doing up here?" he said. "You could've gotten your blond head blown off."

"I knew you wouldn't shoot at shadows," Betsy said as she pushed to her feet and came toward him. "You're the alert kind, not the nervous kind."

"You're going to outsmart yourself one of these days," he grumbled as he slid the Colt back into the holster.

"Not tonight," she said as she dropped to her knees beside him and pressed her palms against the smooth nakeddness of his chest, slowly sliding them across the powerful pectoral muscles, down onto the hard, flat abdomen. Betsy's eyes stayed on his as her lips dropped open.

"You grateful or hungering?" he asked.

"I don't know and I don't care. But I know what I feel," she said.

"And you don't have to think." He smiled.

"That's right," she said, and her hand went to her shirt, began to pull open buttons.

"That's good enough for me," Fargo said on one elbow as she pulled the shirt off. He took in her breasts as they spilled forward, as round and high as they'd seemed under the blouse, the moon lighting pale-pink tips on pale-pink areolae. She wriggled, twisted, and the rest of her clothes came off and she was naked before him, slightly chunky, short-waisted, but a body all curves and roundness and exuding a vibrancy that reached out with its own excitement. A rounded belly curved down to a puffy little pubic mound hardly covered by a blondish nap of tangles and twists. Strong, firm thighs avoided being heavy by having the smooth vigor and bloom of youth. She came forward, pressed herself atop him, and he felt himself rising, responding, stiffening against her round belly.

Betsy's mouth came down hard on his, her lips opened, drawing him into her, sucking, pulling, and he felt the excitement of her coursing around him. Her skin was a warm, clinging sensation, and the short legs moved to slide up along his powerful thighs. "Jesus, oh, Jesus," Betsy murmured as his maleness caught up between her thighs, and she half-turned, came down, and tried to push herself onto him. He rolled her onto her back and she cried out as his mouth took first one, then the other very round breast.

"Slow down, girl," he breathed as he caressed one pale-pink tip with his tongue, drawing a moist circle around the edge of the pink areola.

"Oh, oh, Jesus, no . . . no, hurry, hurry," Betsy cried out, and her chunky body arched, came down on her rear, her legs falling open. "Please, please," she gasped as his hand moved down to rest upon the puffy little mound. He slid his fingers downward, curled the tips around the edge of the triangle, and felt the warm wetness of her spilling out, desire made real, the nectar of the flesh, and he felt his own excitement spiral. Betsy's hand came up to push against his arm, and his fingers slid into the moistness of her and she cried out with a short, sharp paean of pleasure. "Ah, ah, yes, yes, more, more, quick, Fargo . . . oh, quick," Betsy gasped, and her body shook, lifted, all the vibrancy of her shimmering and the urgency of the flesh impossible to deny.

He came over her, slid forward, and she called out with a long, singing sound of ecstasy as flesh touched flesh, pleasure fed pleasure, pure ecstasy entwined, and individual passions became one, flowing together in a spiral of sensation.

Betsy's strong, shaking torso suddenly lifted and he felt her legs clamp hard against his buttocks. "Now, oh, God, now," she half-screamed, and he heard his own groaning sound as he let himself explode with her, felt the seizing, devouring moment shut out all else, the world standing still and all the time capsulated into a single, shining instant. He sank down with her as the long, sighing sound came from her and she collapsed under him, the very round breasts against his face. He heard her sharp, almost harsh breathing and she finally drew a long sigh and held herself close to him.

"You even make love hard-nosed," Fargo commented.

"Just too much wanting all exploding at once," she said. "Give me another chance."

"My pleasure," he said, and she half-turned, pressed one very round breast against his lips. He caressed the tiny tip with his tongue, soothed first, then slowly began to excite.

Betsy responded at once and he felt her hands digging into his back. He let his lips move down from the round breasts, across her rounded torso, tracing a fiery path with his tongue down over the convex mound of her belly, into the tangly curls. "Oh, Jesus," Betsy screamed out. "Oh, good God."

He felt her pelvis thrust upward, her firm, strong thighs lifting her body in a shuddered offering. "Take me, oh, please, Fargo, take me," she gasped, and her hands dug into his back, pushed down his leg, tried to find his pulsating organ. She half-turned, firm thighs wide apart, the eternal offering given up with desire and delight, thrust upward at him, an echo of the pugnaciousness that was part of her. "Now, now, now, damn you," Betsy gasped out, and he slid into her again, more slowly this time, and her groaning sigh was a long, wordless hymn of pleasure.

He held her back longer but not by much as her exploding wanting refused denial and she finally lay beside him, her chunky body still heaving with the last, grasping moments of fulfillment. She took his hand, pressed it hard against the almost-blond, tangly nap, and held it there until she finally drew in long, even breaths and turned to press herself against him. "I never will learn to go slow, not really," she murmured. "I can't."

"I know, you don't think, you feel." He laughed. "Not exactly the same but close enough."

"Close enough," she murmured, snuggled against him. "Let me stay," she said.

"No," he said. "Go back down to the others. Be there when they wake."

"Do you care that much what she thinks?" Betsy asked, lifting her head to frown at him.

"No, not that way," he answered. "But I care about

the truth. I brought you along because you needed help. I don't want to put the wrong face on it."

"I guess you're right," she murmured, and sat up, began to pull on clothes. She finished, leaned over, and hugged him with a quick, impulsive gesture. "You're really something special," she said.

"Go back as quietly as you came," he growled at her, and watched until she vanished down the passage through the rocks. He stretched out, drew the bedroll around himself, and slept in moments, more than satisfied.

He slept soundly through the night and woke when the warm sun swept over him. He dressed and wandered down the rocks slowly, halted at the edge where he'd left the Ovaro, and used his canteen to wash. He smelled good strong coffee brewing and saw Hilda Temple had a big, old baked-enamel pot on a slow fire. He started toward the woman and saw Betsy step from the trees looking smugly fresh, move toward him. "Sleep well?" he asked blandly.

"Very well," she answered, and fell in beside him. He continued toward Hilda Temple when Ruth came from the Conestoga. She'd changed the brown dress for a light gray one of almost the same style, and he saw the icy triumph in her brown eyes as she halted in front of him. Her eyes went to Betsy with disdain.

"It's satisfying to be right, I'll admit," she said.

"What's that mean?" Betsy frowned.

"If you're not his private little trollop, you're doing a very good imitation," Ruth Temple said. "I saw you coming back last night."

Fargo caught Betsy's glance at him and he kept his face almost expressionless as he met Ruth's eyes. "You make a career of spying, honey?" he asked mildly.

"I wasn't spying. I couldn't sleep well last night and I happened to be awake when she came back. I heard her," Ruth snapped, and tossed him a smile of icy smugness. "I just couldn't make myself believe she was out picking blueberries," Ruth said.

Betsy's voice spit out words before he could answer. "Bull's-eye, sweetie. I was out getting laid," Betsy said. "Which is what you wish you'd been getting."

Fargo saw Ruth's face stiffen. "How dare you? I don't wish any such thing," she said, and he heard real protest in her voice.

"You don't even know it. That makes it worse," Betsy snapped. "I'm going to get some coffee," she tossed back as she strode away.

Fargo waited and met Ruth's eyes as she turned to him and he saw tiny dots of color in her cheeks.

"I trust you have the common sense not to believe an outrageous remark like that," she said.

"Tell you what, Ruthie. I won't give it another thought if you don't," Fargo said, and saw her swallow, stare at him, and stride away with her lips a thin, almost bloodless line.

He went over to where Hilda handed him a tin cup of strong, rich coffee with a pleasant smile.

"So much for keeping the right face on things," Betsy remarked.

He shrugged as he drank quickly. "Sometimes things work, sometimes they don't," he said. Will Temple appeared and Fargo set down his coffee. "Don't take too long over breakfast," he said. "I want to move out soon." The man nodded and Fargo walked to the Ovaro, checked the horse's feet, used a hoof pick from his saddlebag to clean out trail crud, tightened the cinch, and was astride the sturdy back as the others began to get their things together. He saw Ruth tending to a latch on the tailgate of the Conestoga and she glanced at him as he called out. "You head due north on this path. I'll come back for you within the hour," he said. "I'm riding alone," he said at the question in Betsy's eyes, and put the pinto into a canter.

He took the path, stayed on it for a hundred yards or so, and swerved up into the high land where juniper and white fir began to grow amid the rocks. He halted after he'd gone on for a half-hour, rested atop a ledge, and scanned the hills, saw nothing move, and slowly turned back the way he'd come. He knew better than to assume the Shoshoni were not out there because he'd picked up no movement. But there was no major war party near or he'd have detected that, and he was glad for small favors.

He rode down and met the wagons, swung in front of them, and led the way up a wide track he'd noted that held good solid earth underfoot. He kept the wagons rolling until the sun had passed the noon sky, and at a small trickle of a stream, he called a halt.

Ruth had bowed to the heat by opening the top buttons of the high-necked dress, he saw, and Betsy rested back where Thomas and Hilda Temple sat with Thomas Junior and Denny. Fargo let them rest, refresh themselves, take on cold water from the stream.

He rose, finally, swept the three wagons with a glance. "We're going to do some practicing before we go on any farther," he said, and drew curious stares. "You'll learn why I had those extra rifles brought along and how you'll be using them." He rested one foot on the step of the first Conestoga as he motioned to the two boys. "Bring the rifles out while I start explaining," he said, and the boys hurried into their wagon. "There's not enough of you to fight off a real Shoshoni attack, or any good-sized attack by anybody," he began. "So we've got to make each of you into four fast-firing riflemen."

"How can you do that?" Amy Temple asked in a querulous voice.

"By making it so that those of you who are shooting don't have to reload," Fargo said. "Without needing to reload, a single rifleman can lay down a pretty damn good barrage. So three of you are going to do nothing but reload the rifles. The others will start with five fully loaded rifles at their sides. As soon as they empty one, they grab the next, empty that, grab the next, and keep firing. By the time they reach the last rifle the first ones will have been reloaded and they just grab one and keep on firing."

"Sort of a round robin of shooting and reloading," Ham Saunders said. "Only without a break in the shooting."

"You've got it," Fargo said. "Without having to stop to reload, each rifleman will equal the firepower of five. Now we're going to practice, and practice hard but without using up ammunition."

"Here are the extra rifles, Fargo," Denny called out as he set the canvas sling on the ground.

"Tom Junior, Denny, and Amy Temple will do the reloading. The rest of you'll be shooting. Now, get under those wagons, riflemen in the front, reloaders behind," Fargo said. "I want you to go through every motion as you would for real. Pull those triggers, put the rifles aside when they're empty, take up the next one. You boys and Amy go through the motions of reloading, exactly as you'll be doing it. Let's start now."

He stepped back, watched as the others flattened themselves beneath the wagons and began to go through the motions of mock firing and mock reloading. He kept them at it, and his eyes swept back and forth, watched each figure closely, took in every motion, studied every movement of hands, bodies, legs. "Faster at the reloading," he barked at one point. "You're moving back and forth too slowly," he said at another. "Keep down back there, keep down," he snapped at another. When he called a halt, they were all perspiring, drawing in long breaths. Only one had been a disappointment.

"Denny, you take Charlotte's place," Fargo said. "You reload, honey," he said to the girl as she looked up at him.

"Why?" she asked, more curiosity than resentment in her voice.

"You don't go from rifle to rifle smoothly enough," he said. "You'll take too much time to keep firing. You'll do better reloading."

She shrugged. "You're the boss," she said, and slid back as Denny took her place.

Fargo had them go through another practice session and was satisfied at his decision. Denny moved with unbroken smoothness, the boy a natural with a rifle, and Charlotte did fine at reloading where speed and not smoothness counted.

"Enough," he said finally. "We'll have another run-through tomorrow. Now, let's roll."

He paused as he passed the first Conestoga.

Ruth crawled out from beneath, the neckline of her dress open enough to reveal the slow curving swell of her modest breasts. She halted, the severity gone from her face for a moment and the natural attractiveness of her almost surprising. "I'm impressed," she said, and made the words sound like an accolade. "A quite imaginative approach."

"It better be a hell of a lot more than imaginative. It better work," Fargo said gruffly. He went to the Ovaro and Betsy came up on the sturdy-legged brown mare.

"You still riding alone?" she asked.

"You can ride with me for now," he said, and she swung in beside him as he waved the three wagons on. "You did well," he told her. "They all did, even Charlotte. I thought she might object to my switching her around, but she didn't."

"Charlotte won't object to anything you do," Betsy sniffed. "She's a firecracker waiting to explode, and she'd like to explode with you."

"More feelings?" Fargo laughed.

"That's right," Betsy said.

"Maybe," he allowed, remembering Charlotte's brief visit. The girl did smolder.

"There's more. Charlotte doesn't want any part of this whole thing. She wants out, and she figures you might be that for her," Betsy said.

"Feelings are one thing, imagining is another," Fargo said.

"I don't imagine and I don't think. I feel, I told you," Betsy said with a rush of pugnacious pride.

"I know, and you trust what you feel. Always," he said, and she nodded with quiet smugness. "Just ride," Fargo said, and sent the pinto into a trot.

He found a place where the rocks narrowed just enough for the wagons to pass through but where the land leveled off. He waited and waved them on when they rolled into sight. He spurred the Ovaro forward as the small caravan slowly rolled through the narrow passage, took a sharp incline up to a high ledge bordered by junipers. Betsy's sturdy mare managed the incline without trouble, he saw, and she drew up alongside him. His eyes were narrowed and his jaw had set tight as he swept the land behind them with a hard gaze.

"What is it?" Betsy asked.

He pointed to a ridge behind them and she saw the long, thin spiral of dust that rose almost straight up into the air. "Shoshoni?" she asked.

"No," he said tightly. "They wouldn't be raising that much dust."

"Somebody coming after us?" Betsy asked, and he nodded, his lips pulling back in a grimace.

"Been afraid they might," he said. "That beer-bellied bastard that played your Uncle Zeb knew my name. It wouldn't take much to put two and two together and find out if a wagon train had set out. Picking up our trail would be the easiest part." His eyes stayed narrowed as he watched the spiral of dust move slowly toward them. "It'll be dark soon and they'll hold up until morning. I figure they ought to reach us by about noon tomorrow. From that dust plume, I'd guess there has to be fifteen or twenty of them."

Betsy frowned at him. "Why so many just to get me?"

"I'd guess they're coming ready to make sure there's nobody left around to ask questions," Fargo said.

Her gaze went out to the spiral of dust again. "Maybe it's just a posse riding on their own trail," she offered.

"Maybe." He nodded. "But I wouldn't bet on it." He turned the pinto from the ledge and rode down to meet the wagons as they emerged from the narrow passage.

Betsy followed in silence as he found a place to camp as the dusk rolled over the foothills. "You going to tell the others?" she asked as they unsaddled and Hilda Temple put on warmed-over stew.

"Tomorrow," he said. "There's always time for bad news." He paused, turned a hard gaze on her. "And I don't want any visits tonight. You get all the sleep you can."

She nodded and strolled quietly away from him. He fetched some of Hilda Temple's stew and sat by himself as he ate. Betsy sat with Will and Amy Temple, he saw, while Ruth took her plate into the Conestoga. She somehow magically reappeared when Charlotte sauntered over to him.

"You sleeping outside of camp again tonight?" she asked.

"Not far enough outside for what you're thinking, honey," he said.

Her pouty face slid into a slow smile. "You don't know what I'm thinking," she said.

"Want to try again?" he asked, and the little smile stayed.

"Maybe some other night," she said.

"Maybe," he allowed, and she strolled away. She'd admitted nothing but she sure as hell hadn't denied anything, either, he smiled to himself.

Ruth passed her as she went away, and Fargo rose to his feet as the tall, willowy form halted in front of him.

"Charlotte's a very young girl," Ruth said severely.

"Not that young," Fargo remarked mildly.

"I want you to stay away from her," Ruth said.

"She's been paying the visits," Fargo said.

"Then you send her away," Ruth snapped.

"That wouldn't be polite," he said.

"You're not going to make this into one of your fruit salads," Ruth flung at him.

He smiled cheerfully at her. "You afraid I won't include prunes?" he asked.

Her hand came up in a short arc that he easily pulled back from, and the slap missed his face by a wide margin. "You are an infuriating man," Ruth hissed. "Your only saving grace is that you are obviously very good at what you do."

"At everything I do, Ruthie." Fargo smiled.

She spun and stalked away, her hands clenched into fists, and he turned and took his bedroll just outside the edge of the campsite. He wondered idly about how right Betsy was about Ruth Temple. Maybe everything was just another form of being in charge to her. Having her way, having others bow to her, was a lifelong habit now. Maybe it was time to change that, he mused. Under that severe facade she was a damn attractive young woman. But then maybe the facade went all the way through. In that case, it wasn't worth finding out. Anyway, it was looking less and less likely that he'd be doing that, he reminded himself as he thought about the spiral of dust. There'd be more than one kind of eruption tomorrow, he was certain.

# 5

He moved the wagons out in the hot morning sun and kept his silence, which drew a questioning look from Betsy that he ignored. Finding a slope studded with clusters of juniper, Fargo led the wagons up into the high foothills, rode ahead, scanned the land in front of them and behind, and still rode in silence.

When he let the horses stop at a thin, mountain stream, Betsy swung alongside him, her voice a strained whisper. "You haven't said anything to them yet." She frowned. "Why not? What are you waiting for?"

"Three things," he said mildly. "One, to be sure we are still being followed."

"Are we?" she asked.

"We are," he said. "They're coming on fast. Two, I wanted to find a place to make a stand. This'll do right here, on the other side of this stream. We'll have that cluster of junipers behind us and they'll have to come up from below at us."

"What's the third thing?" Betsy asked.

"I don't want to leave much time for arguments when I tell them. I figure we've only a half-hour before we have company," Fargo said. He turned in the saddle and called out to the others. "Cross to the other side of the stream and line your wagons up. Overlap them, no wide spaces in between. Line up against that thicket of junipers."

Ruth Temple glowered at him as she moved the lead Conestoga over the stream.

He waited, watched them line up properly and then he swung from the saddle. "You'll be getting a chance to put practice into action sooner than I expected," he said.

"Indians?" Hilda asked with instant alarm.

"No, but there's a posse of gunslingers coming after us," Fargo said.

"Bandits?" Ruth asked. "Highwaymen don't usually bother wagon trains. They want something with more money."

"Usually," Fargo said.

"You think they're bandits?" Ruth pressed.

"Not exactly," Fargo said, and winced inwardly.

"Then, what are they after us for?" she insisted.

Betsy's voice cut in and Fargo saw Ruth turn to stare at her with a mixture of ice and reproach. "They're after me," Betsy blurted out.

Fargo saw the others follow Ruth's stare. "And me," he put in. "Fact is, they're coming after all of you now."

"What do you mean? What is all this about?" Ruth tossed at him.

"I'll explain later," Fargo said.

"I demand an explanation now," Ruth snapped.

Fargo's eyes grew hard as he leveled a stare at her. "You want to hear about it later you get ready to shoot now," he said. She grew silent but her scowl stayed. He turned to the others. "Everybody under the wagons, everything just the way we rehearsed it yesterday," he said.

As the others hurried to obey, Fargo pulled the big Sharps from its saddle holster, watched everyone take their positions, the four extra rifles next to each, those assigned to reloading close behind the first row. He crawled under the Texas cotton-bed rig alongside Betsy and put the rifle to his shoulder. He saw the dust, now a cloud, as the riders raced up the slope, only a few hundred yards away.

"My first shot's going to be for Uncle Zeb," Betsy muttered.

Fargo's gaze stayed on the slope as the riders came into sight and he saw that he'd guessed right as he quickly counted off twenty horsemen.

"I see Ben Brookings," Betsy said. "On the light chestnut."

Fargo picked out the horse and saw a tall man astride it with a tan stetson sitting atop a strong face, beetling black eyebrows, and a square, jutting jaw. "That doesn't leave much doubt now as to who had your Uncle Zeb gunned down," Fargo commented just as he saw the horsemen suddenly slow.

"Maybe he's going to try to bargain for me," Betsy said.

"I'm not going to let him do that—not now, anyway," Fargo said, raised the big Sharps a fraction of an inch, and let his finger tighten on the trigger. The rifle barked and one of the horsemen toppled from his saddle as though he'd been yanked sideways by an invisible rope. The others instantly exploded into action, charged forward just as he had expected they would, with reckless confidence.

"Fire!" he shouted, and the first volley hurtled from beneath the wagon. It became not a volley but a furious, continuing barrage of fire as rifles were switched with hardly missing a beat. It was working perfectly and he felt a grim satisfaction.

The riders recoiled, milled for a moment, and then broke and ran, but not before leaving at least six dead on the ground. They raced down the slope and out of sight, and Fargo crawled from under the wagon and pulled Betsy with him. He waited as the others crawled out, and their faces held a gamut of expressions: uncertainty, relief, apprehension, excitement on the part of the two youngsters. But Ruth's eyes mirrored only icy determination.

"Have they gone?" Amy Temple asked.

"I wouldn't expect so. But they were hit hard. They'll hang back for now," Fargo answered.

"I demand some answers, Fargo," Ruth cut in coldly.

"They want Betsy dead. They already did in her uncle. That's why I brought her. I figured this would be the safest place for her," Fargo said.

"Knowing that unscrupulous killers would be coming after her? How could you?" Ruth accused.

"I didn't know they'd be coming after her," Fargo answered. "I was wrong on that."

"They wouldn't be after us if she weren't here. She's a liability," Ruth snapped coldly.

She was being cruel as well as harsh and Fargo saw the others looking on, their faces mirroring uncertainty. He had to hit back hard, something with enough shock to break off her icy attack.

"You saying I should turn her over to be killed?" he tossed at her, and heard the murmur of dismay sweep over the others.

"I'm sure Ruth doesn't mean that," Will Temple said.

"What in hell does Ruthie mean?" Fargo said, his eyes holding on her. His spearing question had set her back for an instant, he saw, but she recovered quickly.

"I don't want to turn her over to be killed, but I certainly don't want us killed because of her, either. Or because of your mistake in judgment," she snapped.

He smiled inwardly as she came back with the kind of reasonableness it was hard to counter. He decided to fight with the same weapons. "Fact is that it's a bad turn and we've got to make the best of it and that means fighting back."

Ruth cast a disdainful glance at him. "It's a bad turn you brought on."

"Not on purpose," Fargo said.

"I don't believe that counts for much," she sniffed waspishly, and he cursed silently. She was right, of course, and enjoying every damn minute of it. Will Temple's voice cut into his thoughts.

"Fargo's right. We have to make the best of it. We can't toss this poor girl out to be killed," the man said. But Fargo saw Ruth's eyes hold on him with unwavering hardness.

"Some other way out of this will have to be found, and I'll expect you to find it, Fargo," she bit out, turned on her heel, and strode away.

Fargo turned to the others. "Let's move out. No sense in wasting the afternoon," he said, and pulled himself onto the Ovaro. He rode on ahead and Betsy came up to him on the sturdy-legged mare.

"She's right, you know," Betsy said soberly. "They'll maybe all be killed because of me."

"Shit," Fargo snapped. "You, too? You want to go to Ben Brookings and join your Uncle Zeb?"

"No, but it doesn't seem fair," Betsy said.

"Hell, nobody said anything about fair. Killing your Uncle Zeb wasn't fair. Life's not fair, it's real. Fair's a word. Now ride and stop beating on yourself," Fargo said angrily.

She took in his words, he saw, but the unhappiness stayed in her face. She had her own sense of things and he didn't blame her for it, but he'd lived long enough to believe in what he'd told her.

He spurred the pinto forward, explored the long slope, and saw the junipers growing thicker, turning from clusters into a mountain forest. The afternoon was only half over when he drew the wagons into a space inside the juniper forest growth. He formed them into a half-circle and swung to the ground. "Settle down and get some sleep," he ordered.

"Now?" Ham Saunders asked.

"Now. It's hot enough and you're tired enough. I want you awake, come night," Fargo said. He set a quick example as he found a spot, stretched out, and drew sleep to himself. Dimly, he heard the others settle down and he stayed asleep until he felt the night wind brush his face. He woke, sat up, and saw Betsy first, sitting against the wheel of the Texas cotton-bed, awake, knees drawn up.

"Still being a damn fool?" he muttered as he stepped over to her.

"Still feeling guilty, if that's what you mean," she said.

"You'll learn to live with it," he said.

"Maybe I won't have to worry about that. Maybe none of us will," Betsy said glumly.

He turned, clapped his hands sharply, and heard

the others awake, slowly emerging from the wagons. They gathered around, their eyes on him. "Put your bedrolls half under your wagons. Stick a hat on one or two," he said.

"You expect they'll be coming under cover of the night," Ruth said.

"And we're going to be up on the slope. Nobody's going to be under the wagons, where they'll expect us to be," Fargo said. "Take your rifles, no switching, this time. Two rifles for each of you. Lay down flat in a half-circle so you can cover the wagons. Nobody shoots until I do. Then pick your targets." He stepped back and watched as the others took rifles and moved up into the junipers, waited until they were all flattened on the ground.

He moved around the perimeter of the prone figures, and satisfied they were almost impossible to spot, he backed to the side, faded into the brush against a pair of junipers. Brookings would wait until he felt the camp was asleep, Fargo mused, and glanced up at the moon overhead through the slender twigs. Another half-hour, he grunted to himself, and settled down to wait.

His eyes moved across the dark slope and he saw the slender form move a dozen yards from him, rise up on both elbows, and he glimpsed Charlotte's loose, full hair as she moved restlessly. "Stay flat, dammit," he said, his voice a hoarse whisper. She dropped down instantly and lay still.

The half-hour passed quickly and began to go toward the hour mark when he heard the sound, in the distance, the step of a horse's hoof, then another and suddenly the sound ended. The riders had halted and dismounted. Fargo's fingers closed around the butt of the big Colt and drew the pistol from the holster. The thin twigs of the juniper trees let in enough moonlight for him to see the figures moving slowly toward the wagons, crouched low, two rows of them. They spread out as they came closer to the wagons. It was too dark for him to pick out Brookings, and he watched the men steal still closer to the three still and silent wagons.

As he watched, the first row dropped to one knee, raised their rifles, and the second row stayed standing as they brought their guns up. He thought he glimpsed the tan stetson at the far end of the last row as the man raised one arm, brought it down in a quick, chopping motion. Both rows of gunslingers fired at once, one pouring bullets under the wagons, the other firing into the wagons. They stopped after the fusillade and Fargo saw the erratic pattern of tiny holes in the canvas of all three wagons. As the gunslingers halted, peered at the wagons, he took aim at the nearest figure. The big Colt resounded and the figure seemed to do a strange little dance before it fell.

The explosion of rifle fire from the slope followed his shot, and he saw at least three more of the attackers go down. The others dived, rolled away, flung themselves to all sides in panic and surprise as they scrambled to get away. He saw one figure racing in a crouch to the left, almost directly across his path, and he pushed to his feet, darted after the fleeing attacker. The man glimpsed him, half-turned, raised his gun, and fired, and Fargo dropped low as the shot slammed into the tree just over his head. The man started to run on and Fargo rose, kept after him, and refrained from firing the Colt. He wanted one of them to question, maybe hold as a bargaining chip, and he switched directions, drove long, powerful legs between the junipers until he was a half-dozen paces ahead of the fleeing figure. He spun, came at the man, who skidded to a halt in surprise, brought his gun up, and fired. But he fired too quickly and the big figure in front of him was diving low, smashed into him at the knees.

He went down and the big man grabbed at the gun, wrestled it from his grip. "Goddamn," the gunslinger muttered as he tried to roll away. Fargo's arm lashed out, caught him by the neck, and yanked. The man flew back to him, fell at his feet, and Fargo half-jumped backward, but the gunslinger managed to wrap his arms around one ankle. As the man pulled, Fargo, already off balance, felt himself go down, topple forward. Unable to twist away, he came down on his left knee, all his weight behind it as it slammed into the man's throat. He swore as he heard the gurgle of tiny throat bones broken and crushed. The figure twitched spasmodically with a final, rasping sound.

Fargo swore as he backed away. There were no more gunshots. Brookings had made a fast retreat with new wounds to lick. It had been another small victory, but a grim message lay inside it. Ben Brookings wanted Betsy dead. That was damn important to him, as important as it had been to have Zeb Wills gunned down. Fargo put aside even trying to speculate on reasons. The man wasn't going to back away, and he'd be more careful now, perhaps try to pick and choose better opportunities. He'd learned two lessons.

Fargo strode back to the wagons as the others came down from the slope. He saw Betsy to one side as Denny paused in front of him, the boy's smooth, young face flushed with excitement. "We really took them by surprise again. That was great, Fargo," the boy said. "We'll get them next time, too."

"You did well, son," Fargo said. "Now get yourself some sleep." He half-turned as Betsy came to him, her pert face lined with tension.

"There are two young boys who might never get to grow up because I'm here," she said. "It just isn't right."

"We went through that. Forget it," Fargo said gruffly. "Things are what they are. They'll work out. Now get yourself some sleep, too."

She said nothing more as she walked away and disappeared behind the cotton-bed wagon. His attention went to the tall, determined figure that strode toward him. Ruth halted, her face set severely. "I want to talk to you privately," she said.

"Over here," Fargo answered, and stepped to the side of the campsite where the brush grew high.

"They'll be trying again, won't they?" Ruth said.

"I expect so," Fargo admitted.

"We can't just wait around for our luck to run out." Ruth frowned. "Your question was very clever this morning. It made me into a monster willing to throw a young girl to a pack of killers. Naturally the others were instantly sympathetic."

"You brought it on yourself, honey," Fargo said.

"No, I convinced the others on this wagon train I'd get them safely to Picard Flats. That's my first concern, and I won't abandon that," she said.

"I could clear out with Betsy. They'd leave you alone, then," Fargo said.

"And you'd be leaving us stranded here. It's wrong for me to even think of turning Betsy over to those men, but it's fine for you to turn us over to the Shoshoni?" Ruth flung at him. "You have a strange way of thinking. That's an entirely unacceptable solution. You hired on to take us through. You can't just forget about that any more than I can forget about my promises."

"You made your point." Fargo swore silently at the truth in her sharp tongue.

"You find a way out of this, if there is a way," Ruth said. "One that will satisfy me."

"No," he said, and saw her eyes widen. "One that'll satisfy me."

She considered for a moment and turned away, strode back to the Conestoga.

Fargo took his bedroll up the slope and set it down at a spot where he could see the three wagons below and any approach to them. But he didn't expect trouble. Brookings would wait, plan more carefully next time.

Fargo stretched out and felt the weariness hang on him like an invisible cloak, as much inside as outside. Ruth Temple had thrown more than acid words at him. Maybe she'd touched on a truth without knowing it. Maybe there was no way out that would satisfy anyone. He grimaced, turned on his side, and let sleep push away further grim musings.

He woke with the first dawn rays, pulled on clothes, and moved down the slope to the wagons. He'd slept heavily, tired and wanting to lose himself in a few hours of nothingness. The camp still slept, he saw, the wagons silent. His eyes moved over the wagons, a slow, idle glance, paused at the first Conestoga as the rear tailgate flap moved. Ruth stepped out, a nightdress on her tall form that left her bare-shouldered and wrapped itself around her breasts, clinging, outlining her modest loveliness.

She saw him, halted, a moment of startled surprise

flooding her face. She reached into the wagon, pulled a shawl out, and flung it around her shoulders.

"That's better," Fargo said. "I wouldn't want you embarrassing me."

"Amusing," she sniffed, and Fargo's eyes moved across the wagons again. Something was wrong. It had nudged at him in his first glance. He felt the frown dig at him and suddenly his eyes grew wide. The sturdy-legged brown mare was gone.

"Goddamn," he bit out, and saw Ruth stare at him. "She's gone," he said. "Took her horse and sneaked away."

Ruth Temple's frown came slowly. "Betsy Cobb?" she murmured.

"Who else, dammit?" Fargo snapped. "She must've heard us talking last night. She decided to give you that way out you wanted, the one to satisfy you." He spun, took a half-dozen long strides to the Ovaro, and swung onto the horse.

"What are you doing?" Ruth asked.

"Going after her," Fargo snapped.

"No," Ruth said. "It's taken this turn. Let it be. She obviously thought she was doing the right thing."

"She doesn't think, she feels. And she ran because you kept making her feel guilty." Fargo bit out. "Damn little fool. She's not guilty of anything. She's a victim." He wheeled the Ovaro and sent the horse racing away at a fast trot, his eyes instantly picking up her tracks.

She had carefully walked the horse first, he saw, hoofprints neat, evenly spaced. She'd waited till she was at least a hundred yards from the camp before she mounted and put the horse into a trot. Fargo's eyes followed the hoofprints, saw where she'd turned and climbed a steep hill, found a mountain stream, and tried to foil any pursuit by riding the horse through the water. But the stream was shallow and the horse's hooves had splashed a steady shower of water up onto both banks that the new sun hadn't had time to dry away yet.

She left the stream finally as it grew too steep; then she kept moving north through thick stands of white fir and blue spruce, and he followed the prints. They weren't very old, not more than a few hours at most, and he saw where she halted to rest. When she went on, she turned northwest, he saw, and he followed unhurriedly when he suddenly slowed as he picked up the other tracks that appeared from a cluster of spruce, unshod prints of Indian ponies. He leaned forward in the saddle to peer at the prints. They were fresh, he saw, and he slowed almost to a halt as he counted. Three ponies, moving slowly. They had sighted Betsy and were following carefully. They always followd carefully until they were satisfied they weren't being decoyed into a trap.

Fargo reined up as his nostrils flared and he drew in the odor of fish oil and bear grease, the unmistakable smell of Indian. They were close. He slid silently from the saddle, touched the ground on the balls of his feet, and draped the pinto's reins over a low branch. In a crouch, he moved through the trees, followed his nose, and he heard their voices first, grunted words, Shoshonean tongue, and then they came into view. He crept closer as he peered through the foliage. They were dismounted and they had Betsy hung to a low branch by the wrists, her arms stretched up and her feet barely touching the ground.

Fargo dropped to one knee as he scanned the ground in front of him. There were no marks of pursuit. She hadn't heard them until it was too late. No surprise in that, he commented inwardly, and returned his eyes to the three Shoshoni.

They were lithe, strong, young bucks wearing only breechclouts and rawhide belts, and he saw each had a bone hunting knife in the rawhide belt and one also carried a tomahawk. They were busy examining the contents of Betsy's saddlebag, which they'd spilled onto the ground, and one, the tallest of the three, held Betsy's rifle.

They'd be getting around to her soon enough, Fargo knew, but he kept the big Colt in its holster. They'd be easy enough to bring down, but he didn't want to risk the sound of shots. If there were others nearby, it'd bring them on the double. His hand went to the leather calf holster around his leg and he drew out the throwing knife that rested there. Thin, double-edged, perfectly balanced, it was sometimes called an Arkansas toothpick, and he raised the blade in his hand, measured distances, calculated choices and risks.

The one with the rifle in his hands would have to be taken out first. That would leave two young, strong, fast Shoshoni to bring down without using the Colt. His lips drew back in a grimace. He needed to even the odds more. He'd have perhaps six seconds after he took down the one with the rifle, he estimated. That's what it would take them to recover from their initial surprise. But it'd take him at least six seconds to reach the other two. Not enough time, he grunted. They'd be ready by then.

The Trailsman's eyes went to the brush around him. It was high enough. He needed just enough time to immobilize one of the other two. He'd use the six seconds and the terrain and count on their normal reactions, he decided. He steadied himself as he raised his arm, took aim, and sent the thin-bladed knife hurtling through the air.

It hit its mark, embedded itself to the hilt in the Shoshoni's chest, and the bronze-skinned form staggered backward, his jaw falling open at the same instant the rifle fell from his hands. Fargo saw the other two staring at him as he sank to the ground, futilely clutching at the handle of the knife that lay buried deep in his chest.

Fargo rose, leapt forward, and the other two braves spun, saw him as he seemed to start at them, halted, and turned to flee through the trees. He heard their Shoshoni curses as they sprang forward to give chase, and he raced, crouched over, through the high brush, being as noisy as he could. He glanced back, saw both coming after him, bone hunting knives in hand. He slowed, let them gain until they were but a dozen feet behind him and closing fast. He turned away, let himself seem to stumble and pitch forward into the high brush. He rolled, drew the Colt, and came up on one knee as he kept his head down. The two Shoshoni slowed as they scanned the brush for him. One moved toward him, the hunting knife held high in one hand. Fargo held his place a few seconds more, and as the Indian loomed above him, halted, and saw him in the brush, he dived forward and brought the barrel of the Colt around in a long, low, sweeping arc.

The heavy gun barrel smashed into the Shoshoni's groin and the Indian let out a groan of pain. He staggered sideways, fell, one hand clutching at himself. He'd be out of action for a few minutes, Fargo knew, and he rolled in a sideways diving motion as the second brave leapt toward him, brought his knife down in a chopping blow that missed only by inches.

Fargo pushed himself to his feet, holstered the Colt, and let the brave come at him as he moved in a circle. The Indian came in fast, swiped with the bone knife, missed, swiped again. Fargo ducked away, feinted with a left hook, and the Shoshoni's knife whistled up in a sharp lunge that Fargo felt scrape along the knuckles of his fist. The young buck's reactions were fast, too fast, but youth also gave him recklessness. He charged in again, knife swinging in a succession of short, chopping blows, and Fargo gave ground in haste. He continued to back, giving more ground, and saw the Indian forget all sense of caution as he sensed the moment of kill at hand.

The buck drove forward, a sharp lunging thrust, and Fargo had to leap back to avoid the blade plunging into his abdomen. The Shoshoni, his lips drawn back almost in a smile, lunged forward again, and this time Fargo let himself fall as though his foot had caught on something. The Indian leapt, the knife held high to slash downward in a final blow, but Fargo rolled, kicked out with one leg, and caught the brave in the ankle. With a grunt of surprise as well as pain, the buck went down on one knee, but Fargo already had his leg drawn back again. Powerful thigh muscles delivered his second kick high and into the buck's side. With another grunt, more pain in it this time, the Shoshoni went down onto his side and Fargo dived at him, closed one hand around the brave's wrist, twisted, and the knife fell from the man's fingers. The Indian tried to bring his left arm around, but Fargo's shoulder deflected the blow as he rammed his own forearm into the Shoshoni's throat. He heard the man choke for breath and he lifted his arm, slammed it down against the Indian's jawbone, brought all his weight down behind it. He heard the sharp, cracking sound as the man's jaw broke out of its socket, and he leapt to his feet, yanked the Colt out, and smashed the butt down on the Indian's head.

He whirled just in time to see the other brave rising from the high brush, his face still twisted with pain as he charged toward him. Fargo waited, dropped into a half-crouch as the Shoshoni closed in, this time with the tomahawk in hand. The Indian, still in pain, charged low, half bent over, and tried to bring the blade of the tomahawk up in a sharp arc. Fargo pulled away from the blow and brought a hard right around in a sweeping blow. His fist sank into the red man's stomach, and the Indian doubled over. Fargo brought his fist down on the back of the Shoshoni's neck in a tremendous, chopping blow. The brave dropped to the ground, lay facedown, the tomahawk on the grass beside his hand. Fargo picked up the weapon and flung it into the trees as he strode back to where Betsy still hung by her wrists.

Skye stepped to the Indian on the ground, pulled his throwing knife from the man's chest, and a small gusher of red instantly followed. Wiping the blade clean on the grass, he severed the rawhide thongs holding Betsy's wrists to the branch and she sank to the ground with a long, shuddering sigh. He gave her a minute to pull herself together and then lifted her to her feet by one elbow. "Being a damn fool just come naturally to you or do you practice hard?" he asked.

"This is the only way out," she said, summoning up a glower.

"Why not just shoot yourself if you want to get killed?" he asked.

"There's no way out, and I'm not having those people killed on my account," she said.

"You're not killing them. If it happens, Ben Brookings or the Shoshoni will be doing it," Fargo said. "Get on your horse and let's head back before we have more company."

Betsy gathered the things that had been spilled on the ground, stuffed everything back into her saddlebag, and swung onto the sturdy brown mare. She rode beside Fargo in silence.

As they moved through the trees, he scanned the terrain, saw nothing, and didn't feel at all secure. Where there were three, there were more, he muttered. He quickened his pace, Betsy stayed with him, and it was a little past noon when he came in sight of the wagons.

He speared Betsy with a hard stare. "No more damn-fool behavior, promise?" he growled. "I won't come to save your little ass again."

"Promise." She nodded glumly.

He rode forward, and Amy Temple and Hilda came from their wagons at once, concern in their faces as they greeted Betsy.

"You're back safely, thank heavens," Hilda said as she and Amy took Betsy with them to the second Conestoga.

Fargo swung to the ground as Ruth strode toward him.

"I see you found her," she said.

"Three Shoshoni found her first."

Ruth halted, and he saw her eyes flicker, a flash of dismay that she quickly pushed aside. "It still wasn't right to leave us," she said.

"It wasn't right to let her go off," he returned, and Ruth made no reply as she walked away. He had some coffee, let Betsy change and eat something, and finally climbed back into the saddle. "We'll move on. We've some of the day left," he said, and he saw Ruth quickly astride one of the extra horses alongside the Conestoga.

Betsy came up to ride near him and he'd just spurred the Ovaro on when he saw the three riders appear over the rise slightly behind and to his left. One wore the tan stetson and one of the other two held a length of branch with a piece of yellow kerchief flying from it.

Betsy rode up to him at once. "What's that mean?" she asked, nodding toward the kerchief.

"It means that when you've nothing white, you make do with another color," Fargo said. "They want to talk."

The three riders came a dozen yards closer and halted, and Fargo saw Ben Brookings' jutting jaw and beetling black brows under the tan stetson. Ruth came up alongside him, her eyes on the three men. "I'll see what they want to talk about," Fargo muttered.

"I'm going with you," Ruth said, and met his quick glance with cool authority. "These wagons are my responsibility."

Fargo shrugged and pushed the pinto slowly forward, knowing Betsy's eyes followed Ruth alongside him. Ben Brookings' jaw grew more rocklike as he and Ruth neared, Fargo saw, and he met the man's cold eyes.

"I don't aim to listen for long," Fargo said.

"Bow out, Fargo. This wasn't any of your damn business in the first place," Brookings said.

"Came my way. It is now," Fargo answered.

"Give us the girl," the man said.

"Forget it," Fargo snapped.

Ruth's voice cut in. "What happens if you get the girl?"

Brookings turned his cold eyes on her. "Who're you?"

"Ruth Temple. This is my wagon train," Ruth said firmly.

Brookings surveyed her for a long moment. "We get the girl and you go your way," he said finally.

"While you kill her," Fargo snapped.

"We just want to talk to her," Brookings said.

"The way you talked to her Uncle Zeb?"

Brookings' face hardened. "I don't know what you're talking about," he said.

"Shit you don't," Fargo growled. "You don't get the girl. Anything else?"

Again Ruth interrupted. "If we gave you the girl, would we have your promise that nothing will happen to her?"

"You crazy?" Fargo barked. "His promise isn't worth steer shit."

"Of course you have my promise, Miss Temple," Brookings answered quickly, his voice suddenly unctuous.

"I want to think some more about this," Ruth said to Brookings. "We'll give you an answer in the morning."

"I guess waiting till morning isn't going to make much difference," Brookings said. "I'll be here one hour past sunup."

Ruth gave him a curt nod and turned her horse away.

Fargo followed, riding tight-lipped till they were far enough away not to be heard. He reached over, curled one hand around the cheek strap of Ruth's horse, and yanked the mount to a halt. "What the hell do you think you're doing?" Fargo growled.

"Exactly what I said back there. Giving myself some more time to think about this."

"There's nothing to think about, dammit," Fargo said.

"I think there is," Ruth said with icy calm. "A gentleman's agreement may just be the way out of this."

Fargo felt the incredulousness sweep over him as he stared at her. "Gentleman's agreement? You out of your damn skull?" he roared. "He's laughing already."

"How can you be so sure of that? He seemed open to reason," Ruth said.

"He had Betsy's uncle gunned down. He has to kill her. That's why he's come chasing her all the way out here. He's afraid she knows too much of whatever he's covering up," Fargo said. "Turn her over to him and she's dead."

"And it's likely we're dead if we don't," Ruth said.

"Likely's better than surely."

"I told you, I don't want to turn her over to be killed, but I'm trying to find a way out."

"You want to believe Ben Brookings will hold to a gentleman's agreement because it'll let you look the other way," Fargo said.

"And you refuse to believe it's possible because you're afraid to take a chance," she threw back.

"No, because I know you can't make an agreement with a mad dog out to protect himself." Fargo pushed his knees into the Ovaro's ribs and sent the horse forward in a fast canter. He reached the wagons and Betsy came over to him at once.

"He tried to make a deal for me, right?" she said and Fargo nodded. "What'd he offer?"

"Lies wrapped in promises," Fargo said.

Betsy's glance went to Ruth as she rode up and steered her horse to the first Conestoga. "She buy it?" Betsy asked.

"She'd like to. I don't aim to let her salve her conscience," he said.

"What happens now?" Betsy asked.

"He gets an answer, come morning," Fargo said. "Let's move on." He turned in the saddle, waved at the wagons, and waited until they began to roll forward. He left Betsy with the others and rode ahead, his eyes sweeping the land in all directions.

Ben Brookings was a dangerous distraction, but the Shoshoni could put an end to all questions and controversy; the Trailsman scanned the distant ridges carefully. No bronzed riders came into sight. He rode on and explored three passages into the high land before choosing the best and returned for the wagons. The Shoshoni Mountains had formidable terrain but they didn't hold the brutal, devouring power and height of the great Rockies to the north, though they were an offshoot. The range fought intruders with its own weapons of dry, arid, and craggy land. With none of the lushness of the great mountain ranges, water became precious and timber stands infrequent.

Fargo held the horses to a slow and careful pace, and as he paused on a flat rock, he saw the movement to the rear that was Brookings and his men following at a discreet distance. When night came, Fargo pulled the three wagons into a camping space bordered on three sides by pinnacled rock formations and where a small stand of joint firs grew in a half-circle.

Hilda Temple instantly began breaking off the thin twigs to begin to brew Brigham Young tea. Night settled over the mountains and Fargo took his bedroll up to a high ledge, then returned for supper. Betsy stayed mostly with Will and Amy Temple, he noted, where she plainly felt more comfortable. Ruth Temple's distance from her own parents wasn't due to Betsy's presence. He'd noted that much before. She had, he decided, pretty much distance herself from all the others, and as he carried his emptied dish back to Hilda Temple, she returned her plate and paused to meet his tight-jawed stare.

"I suppose you're sorry I came along this morning," she said.

"That's right," he said with gruff honesty. "You didn't help any."

"I tried to find a solution." She seemed genuinely hurt.

"All you did was make it worse," Fargo said.

"How?"

"You let Brookings see we weren't together on keeping Betsy from him," Fargo snapped. "He'll smell dissension and figure there might be more of it. It's apt to make him bolder. He'll keep wondering how many of us really want to fight over keeping her from him."

She stared back as his words circled through her, and he saw her lips thin. "I didn't mean to give him that idea," she said.

"What you meant's one thing; what you did is another," Fargo said. "I'll see you here, come sunup." He turned from her and strode away, passed the others as they began to turn in, and saw Betsy fixing her blanket beside Hilda Temple's wagon. He paused, fixed her with a sharp glance. "You better not be thinking about anymore damn-fool notions," he said.

"I promised, didn't I?" she sniffed.

He nodded, felt her hand come out to squeeze his as he went by, and he climbed up into the darkness to find the ledge where he'd set out his bedroll. He undressed, laid the holster with the big Colt at his side, and watched the stars multiply in the dark-blue velvet cloth that was the sky. He forced himself to relax, shake away the tension of the day, but he kept feeling that nothing was going to turn out the way it was supposed to. Perhaps because nothing had so far, he grunted.

The half-moon had begun its slow passage across the sky when he closed his eyes. He was almost asleep when the sound woke him and his hand was on the big Colt at once. He lay still, listened, heard the scrape of a footstep slipping on the steep pathway to the ledge.

He watched the top of the passage and saw the figure appear, loose, full hair blowing gently in the soft night breeze. "What're you doing up here, Charlotte?" he called softly, and she found him, approaching as he slid the Colt back into the holster.

Charlotte halted before him, still fully dressed, her eyes going over his muscled beauty. "Came to talk to you," she said, and lowered herself to the edge of his bedroll.

"You could've talked to me before," Fargo said blandly.

"I didn't want anybody hearing," she said, and he saw her tongue protrude for an instant, move across her lower lip, which thrust out to help give her the sultry expression she enjoyed carrying.

"Talk," he said.

"If we make it to Picard Flats, I don't want to stay," she said. "I want to leave, and I figured you could take me."

Fargo smiled inwardly as he thought of what Betsy had told him. He notched one up for her. "Why do you want out?" he asked Charlotte.

"I never wanted to come in the first place," she said.

"Why'd you come?"

"Didn't have much choice. Ham Saunders and Eloise brought me. I've sort of been their responsibility since my ma passed on," Charlotte said. "Truth is, nobody really wanted to come on this dammed trip."

"Nobody?" Fargo echoed in surprise.

"That's right," Charlotte snapped with a sudden burst of resentment. "Ruth badgered them all into it."

"You want to explain that some more?" Fargo said.

"Her pa could've found some kind of work, but she argued and nagged and pushed until he agreed to make the trip. Same for Thomas and Hilda. They would've stayed where they were, but Ruth convinced them the whole family ought to go together."

"And Ham Saunders?"

"He and Eloise are kin, cousins. His farm wasn't doing well and he kept blaming the land and the weather and bad crops when truth is he's just a lousy farmer," Charlotte said. "Ruth convinced him he ought to try another place and he finally agreed. Ruth's a very strong-minded woman."

"What's it all mean for her? Why would she do it?" Fargo questioned.

Charlotte shrugged and Fargo saw the top three

buttons of her shirt were open and one young, firm breast nudged upward to reveal its slow, lovely curve. "I've always had my suspicions," Charlotte said.

"Go on," Fargo pressed.

"Her older brother used to be the strong one. He ran things, and when he got tired of it, he up and left. He came out to Picard Flats and dumped everything else in her lap. He stuck her with taking charge and I think she's been looking for a way to get back at him ever since."

"So she's bringing them all out here to him," Fargo said.

"That's right, and proving she can do more than he ever did, too," Charlotte finished.

Fargo turned her words in his mind. "It fits. You could be right," he said. "She's one determined gal."

"Being in charge is a habit with her now. So's having her own way. Sometimes I think she'd like to stop, only she doesn't know how to any longer."

"Maybe," Fargo said, and realized that beneath Charlotte's sultriness she had her own set of sharp instincts. "Why do you think Ham and the others would agree to my just taking you back with me?"

"Who said anything about their agreeing?" Charlotte smiled. "I figure we'll just leave."

"I'm going to be bringing Betsy back," he said.

She shrugged. "That doesn't bother me any," she said.

"I'll have to think some about this," Fargo said.

Charlotte leaned forward and he felt her lips on his—soft, warm, sweet—and suddenly the warmth grew warmer, the sweetness grew harsher. He felt her tongue touch his. Her mouth opened wider, invited, pressed, and her arms slid around his neck.

He lay back and she came down over his muscled naked chest.

Charlotte pulled back for a moment, her hazel eyes darkened as she stared down at him. "That's to help you think better." Her hands moved slowly across his chest, down along the bulge of the powerful pectoral muscles. "Jeez," she breathed, and let her fingers trace a little line around his nipples, move down to the hard flatness of his abdomen.

She lifted one hand, brought it to the bottom buttons of her shirt, and flicked them open. Her breasts fell forward, small pink tips on dark-pink circles, nicely cupped, firm and not really very large. She lowered the two soft cups onto his chest and he heard her quick gasp of pleasure at the sensation of touch that coursed through her.

He raised his arms, took her by the shoulders, held her still as the hazel eyes bored into his. "The chances for no are better than they are for yes," he said.

"Thanks," she said.

"Just wanted you to know," he remarked.

She leaned down and her mouth came over his. "For your conscience or mine?" she murmured through the kiss.

"Both," he said, and felt her tongue slide out to caress his mouth. He answered, drew her into his mouth as he slid the shirt from her, his hands closing over her shoulders. She made wriggling motions and the rest of her garments came off. He saw a body thinner than it seemed in clothes, narrow hips, a flat belly, and a modestly curly triangle.

Charlotte lifted her legs up together, brought them around, and came onto him, and he gasped again at the contact of skin to skin. He felt his own wanting respond, rise to come up with warm firmness against her belly, push into the wiry curls below.

"Oh, Jeez," Charlotte murmured. Drawing her legs up at once, she brought them against his hips as she moved her pelvis back and forth, her portal seeking, straining. He pushed up and felt himself touch her, and she gave a half-scream as he let himself rest against the dark warmth. "Oh, Jeez, Jeez," Charlotte breathed as she sank down over him, and he felt the warm tightness of her give way and she half-screamed again, pain as well as pleasure in the sound. But she pushed down harder and he felt her fingernails digging into his forearms. He found one breast, drew it deep into the warmth of his mouth, a surrogate sensation, and Charlotte held still against him and he could hear her deep, gasped breaths. "Oh, yes, oh, it feels so good . . . oh, so good," she murmured, moved her hips, and gave a quick, sharp cry. Her warm moistness flowed around him and she moved again, cried out, only wanting in the sound.

He let her move at her own pace and felt the sweet sensation as she lifted and came down, her small, tight rear hitting against his legs. Slowly, she began to quicken her movements, lift higher, and come down harder. When he rose to meet her, pushing up deep into the dark, delicious funnel, Charlotte cried out with a short, breath-filled gasp. "Jeez, oh, God, oh, so good, so good." Suddenly she was coming down hard against him, her body quickening its wanting, ecstasy seizing control. Her face came down against him, the thick, loose hair falling over his forehead, and he pulled on the modest breast. "Yes, yes, yes," Charlotte cried out, and he felt her leg grow tight, hold hard against him. She screamed into the hollow of his shoulder, the cry unmistakable, made of new ecstasy and the wonder of discovery, flesh finding more than it had ever known before.

"Oh, God," Charlotte said, her breath a long sigh as she slid down atop him, fell over to lay beside him. "So great, so great," she murmured. "Only too quick. Way too quick." His hand caressed her breasts gently and she lifted her arms to circle his neck. "I want more, tonight," she murmured.

"Tomorrow's going to be a hard day's travel. You'll need some sleep," Fargo said.

"I never sleep much," she said. "Once more, please. God knows when we'll get another chance."

"That's true," he agreed. "I never could resist logic." He drew her to him, pressed his mouth about one modest breast, and let his hand slowly trace a path down her body, across the flat belly, and on into the curly tangle.

"Jeez, yes, oh, God, yes," Charlotte breathed, and her thin legs came up at once as he pressed himself over her and let his maleness rest against the curly darkness. She pressed herself against him and he could feel the desire renewed, the instant burning of her flesh at his touch. Charlotte's sultriness surged at once, her mouth coming down hard against his, urging, demanding, and her body pressed hard into him. She let herself savor the pleasure this time, more pliant than devouring, and when she finally cried out again into his shoulder, the sound held more delight than discovery.

He watched the moon through the straying strands of her thick, full hair as she lay half over him, and he saw that the pale, satellite had crossed deep into the distant sky. He pressed one palm against her small, tight rear. "It's past time for you to be back in your bedroll."

She nodded, lifted herself up, and he watched her slowly draw on clothes.

"Tonight happened. It might happen again. It might not," he said. "Don't expect."

"I never expect," Charlotte said with a sly smile.

"Your mother ever tell you you shouldn't lie," he said.

"Charlotte giggled as she disappeared down the slope in the darkness and he lay back, drew sleep quickly around himself.

The remainder of the night stayed quiet, and he woke with the first rays of the new sun, dressed quickly, and hurried down to the wagons. He'd used his canteen to wash and was ready when Ruth stepped from the Conestoga, and the things Charlotte had told him about her flooded over him. They'd not make her any less thorny, but perhaps they offered a way to reach her. Perhaps. He grunted as he saw the ice in the glance she threw his way.

"I think I ought to confront Mr. Brookings alone," she said as she got her horse from beside the wagon.

"Why's that?" Fargo frowned.

"I thought about what you'd said last night, about my having given him the idea that we were divided about Betsy," she said. "I think it would be more forceful if I met him alone and turned down his deal. He'd have no reason to wonder if I were just going along with you. That's what you want, isn't it? To let him know we'll all fight together?"

"Yes, that's what I want," he said as he turned her words in his mind. "You might just have hold of something. You tell him to his face, without me there, and he'll figure you mean it."

"Then I'll be on my way," Ruth said.

"I'll watch you from the hill, just in case he has

notions of pulling something out of his hat," Fargo said.

Her face remained coldly aloof. "If you like," she said.

"It's your ass I'm thinking about."

"I'm perfectly capable of taking care of myself," she said. "And I don't wish my ass added to your thoughts."

She moved the horse forward and he slowly followed at a distance. She was more icy than usual this morning, he grunted to himself. Thorny wasn't the word for her. She was a damn porcupine, with plenty of fire behind her quills.

He watched as she neared the bottom of the slope and the riders appeared, only two this time, the tan stetson easy enough to spot. He halted high on the slope as Ben Brookings rode up her her. He could see Ruth speak first and Brookings listened. When she finished, he answered, and Fargo could see his lips working as he continued to exchange words with her.

Ruth sat stiff-backed, parrying whatever he had to say, and her answers took too much time. She seemed to be trying to reason with him, Fargo noted disapprovingly. It was Brookings who finally turned away, and Fargo waited as Ruth rode unhurriedly back up the slope.

"More talk than I'd expected," he said as Ruth reached him.

"He tried hard to change my mind."

"Anything else?" Fargo questioned.

"Not really, but I'd guess he doesn't intend to give up," she said.

"He's been hurt twice. He may change his mind on that if he gets hurt again," Fargo said, and rode back to the wagons with her.

The others waited with silent questioning in their eyes, and he saw Betsy find him with apprehension in her glance. "We'll be moving on," he said. "There's no more to be said." He turned the pinto northwest and rode forward, paused, let the wagons start to roll, and then went on again.

The land rose steadily but without any real problem places, and it was mostly the dry, burning heat that sapped the strength of humans and horses. They used water sparingly from the extra water casks and came upon little but dried-up streambeds. But as he went forward, Fargo saw the distant riders following, staying far back, yet unquestionably following.

When dusk came, he halted to a flat place backed with rock pyramids and Betsy came to him as he ate the beans and chitlins Hilda had prepared.

"They just going to keep following us?" she asked.

"Maybe," he said.

"Until they find the right spot to try to jump us again," Betsy said.

"Maybe."

"That could take days."

"Maybe."

"That the only damn word you know?" she snapped.

"No," he said. "I think they're hoping to make you so nervous you'll do something stupid. How are those words?"

She glowered at him. "Good enough," she said.

"Turn in and get some sleep. It's not going to get any easier tomorrow." He rose, brought his plate back to Hilda, and saw Charlotte nearby. She showed signs of exhaustion, and he smiled. She'd not come visiting again, not this night.

Fargo scanned the perimeter of the site and decided to risk one more night without special precautions. Brookings wouldn't hurry into losing more of his men. He'd wait and let tensions build.

Ham Saunders appeared as Fargo started to carry his bedroll to the rocks beside the campsite. "Got a minute, Fargo?" Ham asked, and Fargo paused. "Eloise is sick. She doesn't travel well, and between hardly any water and the heat, she's doing real poorly. I wondered if maybe we could only travel a half-day tomorrow."

"Let's see what tomorrow brings. I'll go along with you if it's possible."

"I'd be obliged," the man said gratefully, and Fargo went on to put his bedroll down in a crevice between two rocks. He let the night grow long before he slept, and he woke with the first warm touch of the morning sun on his face. He had the wagons rolling while the sun was still slanting across the hills, and by noon, when the red sphere burned down straight and hard, and he found a trickle of a stream. It was barely enough to let the horses sip and he was grateful for that.

Brookings had been following through the morning, and the Trailsman saw the distant huddle of horsemen through an opening in the rocks. They'd halted, too, waited, and rested under the burning sun. They were in no shape to do any attacking, he felt certain, and he was thinking about calling a halt as Ham Saunders had asked him to do. He rose to his feet and felt his mouth grow thin.

On the ridge to the west, the line of bronzed horsemen were outlined under the blazing sun, most all but naked, only a breechclout around their groins. They sat motionless on their ponies, as though they'd been carved out of wood and placed there. Indian carvings, he grunted grimly, and counted twenty-six of the still, silent forms. The others were all busy tightening harnesses, fixing ropes, and filling canteens. They were still unaware of the forms on the ridge. "We've got us some more company," Fargo said quietly, and the others looked up, followed his gaze, and he saw the shock flood their faces.

"Oh, my God," Amy Temple breathed.

"Are they going to attack?" Hilda asked with instant nervousness.

"Not right now," Fargo said. He glanced across at Ham Saunders and Eloise. The woman's face was pale with a greenish thing. He'd seen the symptom before. Poor travelers found the ride on rolling wagons over hard terrain much the same way some folks felt seasick on the ocean. "We'll be moving on," he said, and met Ham Saunder's glance. "Better sick than dead."

The man nodded as he helped his wife into the big cotton-bed rig.

Fargo moved the wagons forward over dry, hot ground and rode ahead, finding a high path that let him look down at the wagons and across the mountain rocks. The line of bronzed figures slowly turned and rode parallel to the wagons but at a distance. When the ridge they rode brought them closer, Fargo saw the markings on the lead rider, a tall Indian with his chest painted in red and yellow dye. "Shoshoni," he grunted, the markings only a confirmation of what he'd been certain about. When the day drew to an end, he brought the three wagons into the rock-rimmed half-circle where two lone gambel oaks afforded some shade. The Shoshoni had ridden along with them throughout the day, and Brookings' band had followed. By now they had seen the Shoshoni, Fargo knew, but they had stayed content to follow along and watch.

As Hilda and Amy Temple made a simple supper, Fargo called the two boys to him. "Get all the extra pots and pans and all the extra knives and forks," he said. "You, Denny, take the thinnest string you can find and tie the pots and pans together at both ends. Leave about twenty feet of string in between. You do the same with the knives and forks, Thomas."

"Yes, sir," the boys chorused, and hurried away. They wouldn't be finished till after dark, and that was the way he wanted it. He sat back and watched the women clear away the supper plates, and when they had finished, he rose, saw Ruth, and called to her.

"Get everybody together," he said, and she nodded, marched quickly to each wagon.

The two boys had finished tying the pots and pans and the heavy tin flatware as the others formed a half-circle around him.

"I've had these rigged for the Shoshoni. I don't expect they'll try a night attack. That's not their style. But I'm not going to take chances. The string with the pots and pans on it will be stretched across the front of the wagons. The other across the rear. That way we'll know where they are when they set it off. We'll take sentry duty, two-hour shifts, one sentry at the first wagon, one at the rear of the last."

"Where will you be?" Will Temple asked.

"Someplace where I can see and shoot," Fargo said. "Choose your shifts while I rig up the string, everybody except the boys take their turn." He walked away and began the task of laying the string along the ground at an angle to cover the approach to the front half of the wagons. He kept the string on the ground and stretched it taut when he tied each end to a stone. When he finished doing the same for the rear half of the approach to the wagons, he returned to the others. Ham had taken one of the two first shifts, Hilda the other.

"We drew straws," Ham explained.

"As good a way as any," Fargo said, and fastened Hilda with a glance. "You listen more than look. You hear the clang of tin and you can start shooting." The woman nodded soberly and Fargo waited till everyone disappeared into their wagons, Betsy going into Thomas and Hilda Temple's Conestoga. He walked to the end of the wagons, where he saw Ham Saunders taking sentry. Stepping carefully over the thin string, Fargo walked into the night, circled around, and dropped to his stomach. He crawled back under the middle wagon, silent and unobserved, settled himself, and catnapped.

He woke at once as the first two-hour shift ended, and he saw Will Temple and Charlotte take their places for the next shift. He closed his eyes again, slept lightly, woke with the next change in shifts, and returned to sleep again.

The night passed without trouble, as he'd much expected it would. But he had begun the pattern. The others would be more comfortable with it each night that passed.

Using the inner alarm clock that he had mastered long ago, Fargo woke just before dawn came. With the darkness still cloaking the campsite, he crawled from beneath the wagon, let both sentries see him, and brought in the two lines, working slowly and silently. He had everything stowed away inside the big cotten-bed when the sun came up and the others began to emerge.

He took coffee and a biscuit and watched Ruth emerge, her glance at him instantly icy. Her brown hair was still pulled back severely, but as a concession to the heat, she had changed the full brown dress to a skirt and a light cotton blouse of light gray.

"I think we ought to press on as fast as possible," Ruth said. "I know it will be exhausting, but everyone here is capable of standing up to it."

"I'll keep that in mind," Fargo said, and saw Ham Saunders watching. Fargo strolled to the Ovaro, checked the horse's gear, and swung into the saddle as his eyes scanned the ridges and slopes. He waited, watched as the others climbed into their wagons and Betsy came up alongside him.

"Maybe they've gone," she said.

"Maybe the chicken hawk had stopped watching the hen house," Fargo said, and as if they had heard his words, the Shoshoni appeared over the top of the rock rise to the west.

Betsy flicked a glance at him. "You ever wrong?" she asked.

"Sure." He laughed. "I just try not to be wrong at the wrong time. Let's move." He waved an arm at the wagons and cut up a passageway that held a hard-rock surface that was easy on wagon wheels and hard on horses. He moved slowly, glanced back when he had a chance, and saw Brookings' men following. They stayed plenty far back, though, he smiled.

Fargo held the horses to a slow pace until they were off the hard rock and only quickened their pace slightly when they moved across a loose, pebbly surface. He halted at a trickle of water that bounced down from a sculptured pillar of volcanic rock. He let the horses slowly take in the water, one at a time, refilled canteens, and moved on until another, similar trickle of water appeared. This one flowed down the side of a sandstone buttress, and again he let the horses take in the slow trickle, one by one.

The sun continued to blaze down. The Shoshoni patiently rode alongside the wagons at a distance and Brookings continued to follow. Fargo halted under the noon sun where a tall sandstone column afforded an oasis of shade.

Ruth appeared as he sat down on a flat rock, irritation in her face. "I told you we ought to speed up. You're going even slower than yesterday," she said.

"I asked the horses. They disagreed with you," he said laconically.

"How amusing. I told you, we can all stand it, exhausting as it may be," she said.

"I don't like exhausted sentries, even for two-hour shifts," Fargo said.

"I believe that decision should be mine to make," she said.

"Wrong again, Ruthie," he said. "But if it'll make you happy, I'll give you one to make tonight."

"How big of you," she snapped, and turned on her heel to stalk away from him.

Fargo gave the horses another half-hour of rest and finally moved. He saw the Shoshoni move on with him and glimpsed the distant riders to the rear. The Shoshoni stayed on their parallel ridges through the rest of the day and vanished from sight only when dusk came to settle over the mountains.

Fargo spotted a tall rock formation that would serve as a perfect backstop, and pulled the wagons alongside it. When night came, he worked quickly under cover of the darkness and set up the strings again, let Denny help him, and when he finished, he saw Ruth waiting a dozen yards from the wagons.

"You said you'd something to talk to me about," she reminded him crisply.

"That's right, a decision all for you," he said, and leaned over against the tall rock. "I don't know how long the Shoshoni are going to toy with us, but I expect it's going to end soon. You turn these wagons around and go back and it might just keep them from attacking," he said. "All you'd have left would be Ben Brookings and I'd take him on over the Shoshoni anytime."

"That's a totally ridiculous suggestion," she snapped.

"Only if you call keeping your scalp on ridiculous," Fargo said.

"I haven't come this far to go back. You took all that time to rehearse us in using multiple rifles. We did beautifully the last time," she said.

"That wasn't against the Shoshoni," he commented.

"I expect we'll do just as well," Ruth said firmly. "You have my decision. Good night." She turned and started toward the wagons, her slender shape held in tightly.

"Only that's not a decision," he called after her. "That's just more of satisfying yourself."

She halted, as though a stone had struck her in the back. She turned slowly and he saw the dangerous anger gathering in her eyes. "Do you want to explain that remark?" she asked.

"Do I have to?" he returned.

Her eyes narrowed as they held on him. "That's a rotten thing to say."

"It's a rotten thing to do," he answered. He saw her arm come up in a furious arc, and he pulled back as the slap grazed his cheek. She tried again and he caught her wrist, spun her away.

"Bastard," she threw at him.

"They're here because you brought them here, all of them. For your own damn reasons, not for them."

"Someone's fed you a pack of lies," Ruth said.

"I wondered about that. I wasn't sure it was the truth. Until now," he said.

"We're going on, dammit, do you hear me?" she hissed, her eyes dark with fury.

"Suit yourself." Fargo shrugged. "Only don't call it a decision. Nothing this selfish is a decision."

She stared back for a long moment and then her eyes seemed to draw a brown curtain over themselves as she strode away.

Fargo followed her to the wagons and saw that Will Temple and Betsy had drawn the first sentry shift. He crawled beneath the center wagon again and stayed there until the morning dawned, the sun quickly heating the rocks which had hardly cooled during the night. He had coffee with Charlotte and saw Ruth standing alone, apart, her eyes peering into the distance. Anyone else might have seemed lonely. She seemed only icily aloof and controlled. His accusations had reached deep in her last night, struck a place where there was fire and pain But it hadn't changed anything. She'd practiced too long at being in charge, in control.

Fargo turned his attention to the Ovaro and ran his hands over the horse. Satisfied there were no strained muscles or sore tendons, he climbed into the saddle and waved the wagons forward. He expected the Shoshoni to appear on the ridges to the west, and they didn't disappoint him, materializing as if by magic as they climbed a slope only a hundred yards away. Ben Brookings still followed, he noted, and Fargo put the Ovaro into a canter as he rode on ahead.

The sun burned down and the terrain grew more arid, slopes steeper and narrower. The three wagons were able to negotiate the passages he found and they rolled slowly but steadily onward. The day wore on under the draining heat, Brookings following and the Shoshoni moving along to the west. Fargo frowned as he watched the Indians edge closer, then draw away as they continued to stay almost parallel.

When dark came, he set the alarm strings out again and settled himself beneath the wagon. But once again the night brought nothing but calm.

When the wagons rolled forward the next morning, Brookings and his men followed and the Shoshoni appeared to ride parallel to the west. They halted when Fargo rested the horses and went on when he did.

When dusk came, Ham Saunders voiced the question the others were asking silently, Fargo realized. "Why don't they attack or leave, do something?" Ham asked.

"Dammed if I know," Fargo said honestly, and when night came, he found a site for the wagons, set out the alarm strings and the sentries. But once more, the night was completely uneventful, and when Fargo led the wagons forward the morning after, the Shoshoni appeared again and Brookings continued to follow. They were well into the mountain range now, Fargo saw, and they'd be starting down the far side in another three or four days, he estimated. The strange procession became the pattern for each day. The Shoshoni watched their every move but did nothing except stay with them, and Ben Brookings followed behind.

Fargo felt the crease on his brow become an almost permanent line as he came to discard various explanations for the Shoshonis' behavior that passed through his mind. He thought perhaps they waited for the best place to strike, but he jettisoned the thought when the wagons passed through a number of perfect spots. He wondered if they waited for someone, a warrior chieftain to join them and lead the attack. But no one arrived to take command.

The third day had come and gone when Fargo rode out alone onto a high ridge, watched the wagons roll along a flat strip of hard soil below. He swung the Ovaro sharply west, stayed on the high ground, and headed for the line of Shoshoni. He stayed on a piece of flat terrain as he drew closer. They watched him approach, and he slowed as he drew near enough to see the one with the painted chest spear him with hate-filled black eyes. The Indian raised his arm and three of the others behind spurred their ponies up alongside him. Fargo risked riding closer, cast a quick glance back at the land behind him. It would let him run hard if he had to, and he spurred the Ovaro on another half-dozen yards. The Shoshoni moved closer together, watched him as he halted. He saw two raise their short bows, arrows in place, but they waited and the tall one in the lead glanced back along the rocks and ridges behind. He spoke to the others and threw a quick glance at the rest of his warriors. The two at the end of the column peered back across the top of the ridge, barked something he couldn't catch at their leader.

Fargo saw the tall Shoshoni rein his pony in, mutter to the two braves alongside him, and they half-lowered their bows. I'll be damned, Fargo murmured to himself. I'll be a cactus-eating diamondback.

The Shoshoni stayed, their eyes on him as he

moved backward. Slowly, he turned the pinto and began to trot away, casting a glance back to be sure they didn't decide to charge. But they stayed on the ridge and watched him ride away across the high land and go down to where the wagons rolled along below. He rode slowly, his surprise giving way to a kind of grim laughter that was still tinged with disbelief. He reached the wagons just as they reached the base of a long upward slope where a sudden growth of tall Douglas fir offered cool, sweet-scented shade.

Fargo dismounted as the wagons pulled under the trees and the figures spilled out, weariness lining each face. Fargo saw Ruth swing down from her horse and he watched as some of the others glanced nervously into the distance at the Shoshoni on the ridge.

"Got some good news and bad news," the Trailsman said. "I know why the Shoshoni haven't attacked."

Surprise lined every face that turned to him, and he let another small, grim chuckle escape him.

# 6

"They've been afraid to attack," he said, and saw surprise turn to disbelief. "We've been living a kind of charmed life."

"What are you saying?" Ruth cut in.

"We've had unexpected help—not on purpose, but help nonetheless," Fargo said. "Ben Brookings and his men."

"This doesn't make any sense," Ruth said.

"It does if you know the Shoshoni," Fargo answered. "They're always cautious. The worst thing that can happen to a Shoshoni—or to any Indian—is to let himself be trapped. Being beaten, being outmaneuvered, outfought, outsmarted, even taking on a superior force, all those things are forgivable. They make for great stories around the council fires. But being trapped is different. That's a mark of poor leadership, of stupidity, especially when the trap is there to see."

"They think Brookings is with us?" Ruth gasped.

"That's right. They think we have him purposely

holding back there, waiting to trap them when they attack," Fargo said. "We roll on and he follows, we stop and he stops. They figure if they attack, he'll come charging up and they'll be trapped in a cross-fire."

"I'll be dammed," Ham Saunders said.

"I just moved toward them. They started for me but stopped. They thought I was trying to bait them into doing the wrong thing."

"Then it's all to our benefit. We can just go on without worrying about the Shoshoni," Ruth said.

"No. I said I'd good news and bad news. Brookings is a mixed blessing. The Shoshoni won't let themselves be caught in what they're afraid is a trap. But they can't let us go on without doing something. That means they'll try a coup raid instead of a full-blown attack by day."

"What's that?" Ruth asked.

"A coup raid is an especially daring raid, sneaking into your enemy's camp, killing as many as you can, or maybe making off with one of his people. That way they'll avoid getting into a trap and save face by the daring of a coup raid," Fargo explained. "Which means that Brookings' presence has been a mixed blessing. It's held off a full-blown attack, but it's made a coup raid a certainty. It's made all that practicing with the rifles useless. You can't fight a coup raid that way."

"What can we do?" Thomas Temple asked.

"Keep sentries posted. But one thing is important: when they come, stay inside your wagons. Cover the front and back of your wagons from inside. Make them try to come after you. Inside will be your best protection. Now let's make some more time while there's day left."

He turned the pinto and led the wagons forward over what became a series of small slopes, stairlike, each one growing steeper than the one before. But the footing stayed firm and the last slope ended on flat high land where huge blue spruce formed a cool forest. The dusk was beginning to seep down over the crags and he halted the three wagons just inside the front edge of the spruce forest.

When darkness fell, he set out the alarm strings, fastened each end to the trees, and returned to the wagons. A new moon had began to take its place in the sky and he halted and peered out into the night as Ruth spread skirts and blouses over the rear wheels to dry overnight.

"You expect to see them sneaking up?" she asked.

"No way in hell I'll do that," Fargo said. "I was thinking about Brookings. He keeps dogging our tails, even with the Shoshoni there. I guess he's figuring they might go their way sooner or later and he'll get his chance again. Or maybe he just wants to make sure the Shoshoni do his work for him."

"You insist on making the man into a monster," she said.

"He's done that all by himself," Fargo said.

Ruth turned away, climbed into the Conestoga, and Fargo moved deeper into the spruce forest, not taking his bedroll along. The Shoshoni were running out of time. They'd be coming tonight, he wagered, and settled himself down where he had a view of the three wagons from the rear. He leaned back against the thick trunk of one of the tall spruces and let the forest silence close around him.

The new moon offered only the palest light, and Fargo didn't strain his eyes. It was a night when ears became eyes and sounds became objects. He waited, unmoving, his eyes closed. He heard the sentries change at the end of the first two hours and listened to the silence reclaim the night.

The new moon was high in the sky when the sound came to him, the sharp, loud clang of pots and pans banging against one another. The higher sound of knives and forks hitting together followed instantly. The Shoshoni had tripped the alarm strings at both ends, Fargo grimaced as he pushed himself to one knee. He moved forward in a crouch and caught sight of darting figures clambering up the front of the Saunders' wagon. Two Shoshoni started into the wagon and Fargo heard the shots ring out. One of the Indians toppled from the wagon and the other dived away, hit the ground, and started to race to the other end. Fargo halted, the Colt in hand, and saw another Shoshoni running toward the center wagon. The Indian leapt on the tailboard and he was joined by two more that materialized out of the darkness. Shots exploded from inside the wagon and the first Shoshoni fell, hit the tailgate, hung there for a moment, and slid lifelessly to the ground.

As Fargo headed for the wagon, he saw the second Indian fall out, clutching both hands to his stomach. The third one half-leapt, half-climbed out, and Fargo saw he had Charlotte by the wrist. Fargo halted, raised the Colt, and fired, and the Shoshoni's grip on Charlotte was broken as he plunged backward from the wagon, hit the ground, and lay still.

The other wagons were under attack again, shots resounding from inside, and Fargo saw the racing, darting, crouched figures of the Shoshoni moving in and out of the darkness. A sharp scream made him spin and he glimpsed a Shoshoni leaping from the rear of the first Conestoga, Ruth slung over his shoulders.

The Indian hit the ground on both feet and Fargo saw Ruth's head bounce. He raised the Colt, lowered it, and pushed it into his holster, unwilling to risk hitting Ruth. His heels dug into the ground as he raced forward through the spruce. The Shoshoni carried his prize at a half-run as he headed for the Indian pony a dozen yards away, and Fargo drove long legs forward, running at an angle toward the Indian. He saw the Shoshoni see him as he raced from the trees; the Indian swerved and tried to reach the waiting pony from the other side. He had one arm raised, firmly holding Ruth over his shoulder, and Fargo's hand went to his holster, dropped away again. The Shoshoni ran too fast and swerved too quickly to make a clean shot possible. Fargo drove forward, moving to the opposite side of the pony, was but a half-dozen strides from the horse when the Shoshoni threw Ruth across the animal's back on her stomach. He heard Ruth's half-scream, half-grunt of pain as she landed, and the Shoshoni vaulted onto the horse atop her.

Fargo leapt forward, his feet in the air, and he got one long, outstretched arm around the Indian's neck as the man sent the horse racing forward. The Shoshoni, came off the horse over the pony's wide rump. As Fargo hit the ground with his arm still around the Indian's neck, he managed to glimpse Ruth fall from the pony to collapse in a heap on the ground. The Shoshoni twisted his body, drove his elbow backwards, and Fargo let go as the blow slammed into his stomach.

The Trailsman fell on his rump, saw the Shoshoni whirl, a bone hunting knife in his hand. The Indian leapt, knife upraised, and Fargo got his left forearm up enough to block the blow. But the force of the Shoshoni's leap sent him sprawling back, and the Indian was coming at him again, the knife thrust forward as though it were a short lance.

Fargo flung himself sideways and felt the knife rip the seam of his shirt at his shoulder. The Shoshoni fell forward, carried by the momentum of his leap. He hit the ground, rolled, came up again with the knife raised, but Fargo had found the few precious seconds he needed. The Colt snapped out of its holster, fired, and the charging figure stumbled, twisted, and fell forward. The Shoshoni's arm reached out in a last, gasped effort to strike, fell short, and the Indian stretched out on the ground in a quickly widening circle of red.

Fargo spun, saw Ruth pushing to her feet, and was at her side in a half-dozen long strides. She wore a cotton nightdress and he saw the long, slow curve of her breasts swell up at the open neckline. Her hair had come down and hung loosely around her face.

"You ought to wear your hair like that more often, Ruthie," he commented.

"Is that all you can think of at a time like this?" she asked incredulously.

"It's over. They've gone," he said, and started toward the wagons. "Anybody hurt?" he called out.

Heads appeared cautiously from the three wagons.

"Will's got a lump on his forehead, but he's all right," Amy Temple said.

"Charlotte's got a sprained arm," Ham Saunders said. "That's all here."

Ruth came up beside him as he halted outside the wagons.

"We were lucky," he said.

"They didn't expect your shooting from outside," Thomas Temple said. "Will they try again?"

"Not tonight. Maybe not ever again. A coup raid is special. If it fails, it's put aside on its own. It's not part of any pattern of attack. You can sleep the rest of the night." As heads drew back into the wagons, the Trailsman turned to Ruth and saw her eyes searching his face.

"He'd have made off with me if you hadn't been there," she said. "I'm grateful."

"Probably a new feeling for you," Fargo said, and her eyes darkened at once.

"Was that necessary?" she snapped.

"Was it true?"

"Yes," she said as she lifted her chin high. "But I'm still grateful. You'll have to be content with that."

"Wouldn't expect anything more," he said, and she strode away. "Still think you ought to wear your hair that way, Ruthie," he said.

"Ruth," she said without looking back.

Fargo laughed and returned to the spruce forest, this time with his bedroll. He stretched out under the tall, sweet-scented trees and slept quickly. Morning would arrive soon enough, he knew, and the night stayed quiet until dawn brought the first yellow-pink stripes. He woke slowly, allowed himself a little extra time to relax, and finally rose, walked down to the wagons, which were still silent with sleep. He used his canteen to wash and was in the saddle when the others woke.

"Keep some coffee for me," he said to Hilda Temple. "I'll be back," As he rode away, he saw Ruth step from the Conestoga, her hair pulled back in the bun again, and she saw his quick grin and looked away. He spurred the Ovaro up a narrow, steep passage that brought him to a high crag where he could see the land to all sides. He peered back the way they had come the day before and saw Brookings' men as they began to slowly move through the rock formations. His eyes slowly scanned the terrain in a full circle, but the only thing he saw was the movement of Brookings' party.

It was early yet, he realized, but he let his eyes sweep the mountains again. He turned finally and rode back to the wagons as they prepared to roll out. Hilda had the tin cup of coffee waiting for him and he sipped the hot, bracing brew as he rode. When he finished, he tossed the cup to her, and her husband caught it, snapped the reins, and moved his wagon forward.

Betsy came up as Fargo turned the Ovaro to ride on. "Can I come?" she asked and he nodded. She rode alongside as he explored the terrain to the northwest and he halted as he found a wide path that began the trek down out of the rock-filled mountains.

"How long before we make Picard Flats?" Betsy asked.

"Maybe another two, three days," Fargo said.

"What happens afterward?" she said.

"I leave," he said.

"I want to go back. I want to find out why that bastard killed Uncle Zeb and why he wants to kill me. Will you help me? Will you go back with me?" she asked.

He fastened her with a stare that held grim tolerance. "I expected you'd come up with this," he said. "I'll think about it."

"I'm going back," Betsy said. "Whether you come or not."

"There's being hard-nosed and there's being plain dumb," he said.

She managed to shrug and glower at the same time. "And there's not forgetting about a man who was kind and good and gave me a home when I needed it," she said, wheeled her horse away, and cantered back to the wagons.

Fargo swore under his breath, swept the land again and rode on.

He had halted halfway down the long slope when the wagons finally rolled up and the sun started to slip down behind the distant crags. "Pull them in over there," he said, gesturing to a flat circle of land half-ringed by small boulders. He waited till the wagons rolled to a halt in a loose semicircle and Hilda and Amy Temple began to cook supper. "No Shoshoni," he said. "They've gone."

"Will they be back?" Will asked, the bandage still on his temple.

"Maybe. I'm guessing no. If they don't show tomorrow, I'd say they won't be back," Fargo answered. He heard a collective sigh of relief he hoped wasn't premature, and after supper he put his bedroll beyond the ring of boulders in a small niche. He could see the wagons and the land on all sides, and he stayed awake till the night grew deep. He let himself sleep finally, satisfied the night would remain quiet.

He was right. He woke with the new day, swept the terrain with a long, searching glance, rose, then dressed and walked back to the wagons. In the distance, he saw Brookings' men begin to move along the rocky crevices. But no Shoshoni appeared to silently watch and ride along with them.

Fargo led the wagons downward and found a sudden area where drainage from the rocks had formed a soft, sucking base. He halted the wagons at once. The narrow rocky passage around the area took up the rest of the day, and when he found a place to halt for the night on the other side of the soft ground, the sun was sinking fast. He gazed behind the path they'd taken in the last of the daylight and saw Brookings and his men moving tiredly across the harsh land.

The women made supper and he ate alone.

When he finished the simple meal, Betsy came over to him. "You decided about helping me?" she asked, a touch of petulance in her voice.

"No," he answered.

"Maybe I should come visit you tonight and help you decide."

"That'll help me enjoy. It won't make me decide," he said.

"Then you can wait to enjoy," she said, and flounced away. He laughed as he returned his plate to Hilda.

The wagons grew still quickly and Fargo let his eyes move across the dark shapes of the distant rocks and crags as he stood alone at the edge of the campsite. He heard steps behind him, turned to see Ruth carrying a bucket of water from the rear of the Conestoga to the horses. She set it down by the horses and came over to him.

"There were no Shoshoni today again," she said. "I take it that means they've gone."

'I'd say so."

"I think we owe Mr. Brookings a vote of thanks.

"I owe him suspicion," Fargo said. "Why hasn't he tried hitting us? He's had two days now, and there were others before the Shoshoni arrived. He's got to know we're getting damn near Picard Flats."

"Maybe he's given up the whole idea," Ruth said.

"Like hell. He's not come all this way just to let Betsy slip away from him," Fargo said. "He's still following, still dogging our tracks. Why?"

Ruth shrugged. "I'll leave that for you to wonder about, Mr. Fargo," she said, and started to move toward the Conestoga.

"Still think you ought to wear your hair down, Ruthie," he said.

"Ruth," she snapped over her shoulder as she went into the wagon.

Fargo took his bedroll away from the campsite, stretched out on it where he could look down at the wagons, and finally slept as the moon moved across the sky.

Morning dawned still hot and he led the wagons downward into the lower range of the mountains. Ben Brookings still followed behind, keeping his distance, and Fargo frowned as the day came to an end and the man had still made no move to do anything except stay back.

"Sentries tonight," Fargo told the others. "Just as we did before, two-hour shifts."

"You going to string up pots and pans again?" Denny Temple asked.

"No, I'm not thinking about the Shoshoni. Sentries will do," he answered, took his bedroll beyond the wagons and stretched out.

The night stayed quiet and he finally slept until the new day came. He rode downward, the land leveling out by the afternoon, and behind them Brookings still followed. Betsy brought her sturdy-legged mare up beside him and her glance backward was made of nervousness.

"What is he doing?" she asked.

"Dammed if I know," Fargo answered. "We'll reach Picard Flats tomorrow."

"Maybe that's what he's waiting for. Maybe he figures to make a try for me in Picard Flats. Maybe he thinks he'll have a better chance there."

Fargo's frown stayed as he thought aloud. "Might just be the answer. I can't think of anything better," he said. "Maybe he thinks you'll be on your own when we reach Picard Flats."

Betsy nodded agreement and rode along the rest of the day in silence beside him.

Night brought camp down in the foothills of the range where good green gambel oaks were a refreshing sight. Fargo continued the sentries, slept away from camp again, and the night stayed still, with only the distant cry of a wolf to break the silence. When morning came, he stayed with the wagons until almost noon and saw the spiral of dust behind them that told him Brookings still followed though the tree cover kept him out of sight. It was Charlotte's turn to come up to him as he rode slowly ahead of the wagons.

"I still want out, Fargo," she said. "I haven't bothered you any about it."

"That's true enough," he agreed. "You've been real good."

"That doesn't mean I've changed my mind any," she said.

"I'm still thinking on it," he told her, and she accepted his answer and dropped back. He saw Ruth watch Charlotte return to the others with icy disapproval in her face.

The land suddenly leveled off to an almost flat plain and he turned his eyes away from Ruth to peer into the distance. They'd reach Picard Flats in another few hours, he guessed, probably just by night.

"I'm going to go on ahead," he told Will Temple after another hour had gone by, and the man waved back as he put the Ovaro into a trot. He let the powerful horse move in a distance-devouring gait and slowed only when the buildings of Picard Flats came into sight. He rode into a town pretty much the same as most, only it sported a church as well as a dance hall. He moved through slowly, halting before the sheriff's office, where a man sat with a star-shaped badge on a vest that had difficulty closing over his portly form.

"Bringing some wagons in. Name's Fargo," he said.

"We welcome new folks here," the man said. "Always need new people to keep the town growing. Need replacements."

"For what?" Fargo frowned.

"For those who keep wandering too far into the Shoshoni range and those who take off for California," the sheriff said. "We got us a doctor but we can use a barber and a tailor."

"Know a young fellow named Temple?" Fargo asked.

"Rob Temple? He was one of those who went too far into the Shoshoni range," the sheriff said. "Buried him about a year ago."

Fargo's mouth tightened. Name and dates fitted, and he disliked the news he'd carry back. Maybe he'd say nothing, he told himself, let them do their own finding out. "Much obliged," he said and wheeled the Ovaro around, trotted back out of the town.

He met the wagons halfway along the road to town, swung in beside them as the dusk began to settle down. Night came quickly, before they reached town, and he glanced back to see the distant knot of riders still following.

"I think it'd be best if we camp outside of town for the night," Ruth said. "It'll be too dark to go searching for anyone."

"Good idea," Fargo agreed, and the night had blanketed the land when he drew the wagons to a halt a few dozen yards from the first buildings of Picard Flats. The wagons formed a loose triangle, and Fargo peered into the darkness as he stood outside. He saw the figure step out from between the wagons to stand beside him.

"They're out there," Betsy said.

"That's one reason I was quick to agree to Ruth's decision to camp here. I want a better look at the town before you go into it tomorrow." Fargo said.

"What was the other reason?" the voice cut in, and he turned to see Charlotte there.

"Her brother's been dead for a year," he said. "Shoshoni arrows."

Betsy's round, pert face grew sober. "I'm sorry for her," she murmured.

"She'll be as frustrated as upset," Charlotte said, and drew a disapproving frown from Betsy. "I'm not being cold. They were never close and I told you she came out here to get back at him. She won't be able to do that now."

Fargo started to move back to the wagons and both young women went with him. "Get yourselves some sleep. Tomorrow might be a quiet day, but then it might not," he said, and Betsy nodded at his glance. He took his bedroll, stretched it out beneath an oak a dozen yards from the wagons. He lay down, the big Colt under his hand, and finally slept as the night stayed peaceful.

Dawn came to wake him, and he rose on one elbow, blinked away sleep, and looked across at the

142

wagons. Everything seemed quiet and in order, and he rose, went to the last Conestoga, and used the extra water casks to wash. He was finished and dressed when Hilda emerged, saw him, and offered a quick, happy smile.

"I thought maybe we'd get coffee in town this morning," she said.

"Why not?" Fargo agreed as the others began to climb out of their wagons. Ham Saunders and the boys next, then Eloise Saunders, Charlotte following. Amy and Will Temple emerged with a cheerful greeting. Ruth followed and a little later Thomas Temple swung to the ground.

Fargo felt the frown digging into his brow. Everybody but Betsy. He lifted his voice and called her name. She didn't answer, didn't emerge from any of the wagons. "Where's Betsy?" he barked, taking in all the others with his quick glance.

Ham Saunders shrugged. "Haven't seen her," he said.

"She's been sleeping in our wagon," Amy Temple said. "She was there when we went to bed."

"You didn't hear her leave?" Fargo frowned.

"No, but I'm a sound sleeper," Will Temple said.

"I heard Ruth stirring early this morning," Amy Temple said.

"I was having a bad dream. I often talk in my sleep when I dream," Ruth said.

"Did you see Betsy?" Fargo asked.

"No," Ruth answered, and started to turn away.

"That's a damn lie," Charlotte's voice cut in. "You were with her this morning, early this morning."

"You're imagining things," Ruth said, and Fargo's eyes stayed on Charlotte as she turned to him.

"The hell I am. I heard some noise and looked out

of our wagon," Charlotte said. "She and Betsy were walking off together. Betsy was in front and she was right behind her."

"As she'd be if she were holding a gun to her," Fargo said.

"Yes, exactly, though I didn't think anything more at the time. I just went back to sleep," Charlotte said.

"She's lying, the little tramp," Ruth snapped.

Fargo spun and his hand shot out, closed around the high neckline of Ruth's dress, and he yanked her almost into the air. "You took her out of your wagon at gunpoint, didn't you?" Fargo rasped. "You answer me or I'll break your lovely neck." He saw Ruth's face grow pale as fear came into her eyes.

"She's perfectly all right," Ruth said.

"What the hell does that mean?" Fargo roared.

"I turned her over to Ben Brookings. He assured me again that he only wanted to talk to her," Ruth said.

Fargo's hand tightened on the dress and he saw Ruth gasp. "What do you mean you turned her over to Brookings? Is that why he kept following us? You made a deal with him, didn't you? Back when I thought you were telling him off."

Ruth nodded, fought for breath. "Yes," she gasped out. "I agreed that if he'd let us go our way, I'd turn her over to him when we reached Picard Flats."

Fargo forced himself not to further tighten his grip on the girl's throat. "You bitch. You sneaky, lying little bitch," he rasped. "You just murdered Betsy Cobb."

"No, he just wants to talk to her. I asked him again and he promised me." Fargo saw fear and panic in her eyes.

Fargo felt the fury inside him explode and he

flung Ruth Temple's tall form away from him with enough force to send her sprawling across the ground. "I haven't time for anything but going after Betsy," he roared. "But you can be damn sure I'll be back." He ran past her, threw another curse at her, and vaulted over the Ovaro. "Which way, damn you?" he thundered as he reined up inches away from her.

"South," she answered from where she lay. "Down a long ridge."

He sent the horse into a gallop, hooves flinging dirt back over Ruth as he raced away. He found the long ridge easily, slowed, scanned the hard ground, and managed to pick up their tracks where a layer of loose dirt covered the rock beneath. They'd gone down the long, sloping ridge, not more than two or three hours before, he estimated. He followed, swerved left when the tracks moved away from the ridge and onto a clay and sandstone plateau. They were trying to avoid climbing up into the high range, he saw, moving through cuts in the rocks to stay low. He sent the Ovaro racing after the prints, ten horses, he guessed, and followed where they were forced to climb a suddenly steep passage.

He'd ridden for a little more than an hour, he estimated, when he saw the steady trail of prints come to a halt, become a milling pattern of tracks. They had stopped here, but he saw no reason: no stream, no water trickling down from the rocks above, no water hole, nothing but some tough mountain scrub brush. To the right of where they'd halted, the land dropped down in a steep dip.

Fargo's eyes scanned the ground again, traced the patterns made by the horses as they stopped and milled in a circle. The frown came at once to dig into his forehead as he saw the marks that moved from the hoofprints to the edge of the steep dip, long, trailing marks as though something had been pulled across the ground. Something or somebody, Fargo grunted through lips that had become a thin, angry line. He took four long strides to reach the edge of the steep dip and peered down. "Ah, shit," he swore. "Goddamn."

Betsy's still form lay facedown at the bottom of the falloff, and he lowered himself, half-slid and half-climbed down the steep sides to land almost on top of her. He put his head down to her. "Damn, she's breathing," he said, and slowly turned her onto her back. A small stain of red began to spread on her stomach at once. She had landed on a piece of root that pressed up against the bullet hole and acted as a bandage, keeping the blood in.

Working quickly, he tore off her blouse, made it into long strips, and pulled them tight across the wound to staunch the flow of blood that had quickly begun to pour out. She stayed unconscious but she still breathed. He rose, peered around him, and found one end of the deep depression, rose in a less-steep incline. He lifted Betsy, carried her up from the place where they'd thrown her, and laid her gently across the saddle. He climbed onto the horse, lifted her up again, and put her against his chest, almost as though she were sitting in the saddle with him. He sent the Ovaro back the way he'd come, kept the horse at a walk, and wondered how much time she had left.

They'd shot her, tossed her into the small dip, and left her for dead. Maybe they'd still have their way, Fargo grimaced. She'd have died from loss of blood if the piece of root hadn't pressed against the wound.

Maybe her luck would still hold out, he hoped as he rested her face against his shoulder.

The ride back seemed to take forever at the slow, steady pace he kept the Ovaro, afraid that the jarring of a trot or canter would perhaps do more harm. He was perspiring, his face coated with tiny beads that glistened under the hot sun as he finally came in sight of Picard Flats.

The three wagons were still in place at the edge of town and he saw the figures come tumbling out as he reached them. The makeshift bandages he'd tied around Betsy's stomach were no more than that, and blood had seeped through them to turn her midsection red. He saw Amy Temple stare as he went past, shock and horror in her face. The others mirrored her thoughts, everyone watching in silence as he passed. Except Ruth. She was not among them.

"There's going to be no hiding place," Fargo said as he passed by. "You can tell her that. No hiding place." He rode on through the town and saw onlookers stare.

The sheriff hurried toward him as he reached the man's office, his glance taking everything in at once. "This way," the sheriff said. "Doc Frisland's just a few doors down."

Fargo followed the man as he ran ahead. When he reached a narrow wood house with a neatly painted fence around it, a thin man wearing a white jacket was already hurrying outside. A woman began to follow him, but he called over his shoulder to her. "Get the stretcher, Molly," he said, and she disappeared into the house.

Fargo halted as the sheriff and the doctor reached hands up.

"Easy now, get her down slowly," the doctor said.

Fargo leaned his head down to Betsy's face. She was still breathing, still alive. The woman came out with the canvas stretcher and she and the doctor carried Betsy into the house as Fargo slid from the pinto and tethered the horse to one of the fence posts.

"What happened?" the sheriff questioned.

"She was shot and left for dead. Bunch from way the other side of the Shoshoni range," Fargo said. "I know who they are and I'll go back and get them. They've hightailed it by now."

"Nothing in my backyard, then," the sheriff said.

"Nothing," Fargo said, and strode into the house.

The woman met him in a large living room that obviously served as a waiting room. "The doctor's examining her now and she's still alive. I'm Molly Frisland. How far did you have to come to get her here?"

"Couple of miles, I'd guess," Fargo said.

"You related to her?" the woman asked.

"No, but I've been kind of keeping watch over her," he answered. "Not well enough, it seems," he added grimly. "Can I wait?"

"Of course, though I don't know how long the doctor will be. Just make yourself comfortable," Molly said, and went into the next room.

Fargo stared through the window for a few minutes, the anger inside him still a cold, hard knot in the pit of his stomach. He finally sat down on a worn leather chair and felt his hands clench and unclench. He had long ago learned how to wait as the wild creatures wait. He had come to know that waiting was but another part of acting. But this was a different kind of waiting where there was only a feeling of total helplessness, and he cursed silently as time seemed to stand still.

He'd no idea how long he had sat in the leather chair when the door to the other room opened and the thin figure stepped out. Fargo got to his feet at once and met the doctor's grave eyes.

"We may have some kind of miracle here," the doctor said. "She's conscious, though I've given her a sedative. I'm told it was hours ago that she was shot. I don't know why she just didn't die of loss of blood."

"The root," Fargo said, and drew a frown from the doctor. He explained how he'd found her and the doctor nodded slowly. "Amazing. A miracle indeed. She was lucky, in more ways than that. She was plainly shot at close range and the bullet seems to have missed every vital organ."

"Jesus," Fargo breathed.

"She's young, strong, healthy, and she didn't lose all that much blood. I expect she'll be good as new in time. It'll take a while, of course. As I said, she's one very lucky girl," Dr. Frisland said.

"She's a real hard nose," Fargo grunted. "Maybe that's helped her in this. When can I talk to her?"

"Tomorrow," the doctor said. "Come back tomorrow."

"I'll be here," Fargo said. "And thanks."

The doctor nodded gravely.

The Trailsman strode from the house, pulled himself onto the Ovaro, and flipped the reins from the fence post. The icy grimness settled over him again at once as he rode through town.

Amy and Will Temple were first out of their Conestoga when he pulled to a halt.

"Where is she?" Fargo growled.

"Waiting for you," Will Temple said.

"Where?" Fargo barked as the others emerged from their wagons.

Will pointed east to a low crest grown with oak. "Up there someplace," he said.

Fargo started to turn the Ovaro when Ham Saunders called out.

"Betsy? What happened?" he asked.

"She's going to pull through," Fargo said, and fastened his eyes on Will and Amy Temple. "That doesn't change a damn thing," he said.

The man nodded, eyes heavy. "I know that," he said. "But Betsy's going to live. Let it mean something."

Fargo made no reply as he spurred the pinto forward. He nodded at Charlotte as he rode on, and she answered with a flicker of her eyes. The crest with the oaks came up quickly as he put the horse into a fast canter, and when he saw the horse beneath the branches of a wide tree, he slowed, moved forward with the fury churning inside him. He halted as he saw Ruth step from the trees; he slid from the saddle and she faced him with her chin held high, her hair still pulled severely back. But her composed, authoritarian face was stained with tears, her eyes red and swollen.

"Didn't think you could," he said.

"Could what?" she asked.

"Cry," he bit out.

"Is she . . . ?" Ruth began, her voice cracking.

"Dead?" Fargo finished coldly. "No, she's going to make it. No goddamn thanks to you."

"Oh, God, oh, thank God," Ruth said, and sank down to her knees, her hands clasped in front of her, her head bowed. When she lifted her head to him, he saw the tears brimming over her eyes, running down her cheeks. "I never wanted this to happen. I believed him when he said he just wanted to question her," Ruth began.

Fargo's hand shot out, seized her by the front of her dress, and he yanked her to her feet. She yelped, more in surprise and fright than in pain.

"No more goddamn lies, you stinking, selfish little bitch. You made the deal because you wanted to. You looked away on purpose." He opened his hand and let her slide down to the ground.

Ruth looked up at him, shook away tears, and closed her eyes for a moment. "The night before," she said, pulling her eyes open, "I saw Charlotte come back from being with you. I was furious. I hated you for having been with her, and all the things you said. That's when I decided to make the deal with Brookings."

Fargo's brow wrinkled with the frown that dug deep. "I'll be dammed," he breathed.

"It made looking away easy," Ruth murmured, turning her face away from him. "It made believing him easy. But I knew better, I guess, deep down inside someplace. Maybe I wouldn't have done it if you hadn't been with Charlotte that night."

"That's no fucking excuse," Fargo flung at her, and pulled himself angrily onto the pinto.

Ruth looked up, surprise through the tears that still filled her eyes. "Is that all?" she asked.

"You want penance? You want to atone for your sins? You looking for punishment to make you feel better?" he flung at her.

"Maybe," she said, and swallowed hard. "Maybe I just want to do something to make up."

"You can't undo what's been done. Betsy's lucky. She's going to live. You're even luckier for that," Fargo said.

"I just didn't think you'd be finished with me this way," Ruth said.

"I'm not," Fargo said, his eyes hard. "I just haven't decided what I'm going to do yet. Maybe I'll kick your ass all over the territory. I'll be thinking about it, you can be damn sure of that." He started to wheel the Ovaro away.

"I never wanted this. I never meant to have her hurt," Ruth called after him. "I'm sorry, sorry for everything."

"Being sorry is the easiest thing in the world," he threw back at her. "It doesn't help shit." He sent the pinto into a fast canter and rode back to town. He went past the wagons without slowing, though he saw Will Temple outside.

In town, he found the saloon, ordered a bottle of bourbon, and took a table in the corner. He took the precaution of renting a room upstairs before addressing himself to the bourbon again.

It was a time for closing out the world, pushing away errors of judgment, mistakes, envies, and jealousies. But the seething anger would stay inside him, he knew. Not just at Ruth Temple but at a stinking, murdering son of a bitch named Ben Brookings. He owed that much to Betsy. He'd see it through to the finish for her.

# 7

He stared at her in amazement. He'd cleared his head of bourbon cobwebs before arriving at the doctor's office, so he knew he wasn't imagining anything. She was sitting up in the bed, pillows propped up behind her. Except for a hint of pain in her eyes, Betsy didn't look a bit worse for wear.

"Damn hard nose," he murmured as he kissed one round cheek.

"I found out things, Fargo, before Brookings shot me," Betsy said. "I made him think I'd talk if he did. I know just what Uncle Zeb found out now."

"I'm listening," Fargo said, and perched himself at the edge of the bed.

"Brookings has been cheating the government for years with that haulage line of his," Betsy said. "A government inspector is there when the wagons are loaded, usually an army man. He checks the weight and cargo with Brookings, gives the weight sheet to the driver, and the wagon goes out. There's one driver and one helper on each wagon, usually the same driver and helper. Sometimes along the way they meet some of Brookings' men and a quarter of the cargo is taken from the wagon. When the wagon goes on and reaches its unloading place, the weight of the wagon is checked again against the driver's weight sheet."

"That ought to show a big difference," Fargo said.

"Only it doesn't, because Brookings is there with two government men he has in his pocket. They pass the weight off as being the same as on the driver's sheet," Betsy said.

"Brookings gets paid for short-weight cargo and he sells the stuff he's taken off on his own," Fargo said.

"Exactly," Betsy said. "He's been doing it for years and making a fortune."

"That's what your Uncle Zeb found out," Fargo said, and Betsy nodded, winced, and half-smiled apologetically.

"Uncle Zeb made the mistake of telling Brookings he wouldn't say anything if Brookings would find a way to repay the government," Betsy said. "Brookings' answer was to have him gunned down."

"No wonder he was so anxious to get his hands on you," Fargo said. "You were the next smoking gun hanging over him. And now he figures he's taken care of everything."

"But he hasn't. As soon as I get well enough, I'm going back and nail his stinking hide to the wall," Betsy said, started to sit up, and yelped in pain. She sank back onto the pillows. "If you'll still go with me," she said.

"No," Fargo said, and drew an instant frown. "I'm going back to take care of Brookings now," he finished.

"You'll need help. I'll be out of here soon," Betsy protested.

"Not according to the doctor. You've been very lucky. Don't push it," Fargo said.

"Why can't you stay till I'm ready?" Betsy frowned.

"Two reasons. One, I can't wait around that long, and two, news has a way of traveling. If it gets to him in time that you're still alive, he'll come after you again. He's got to be stopped now and I'm going to do it, for us both." He leaned over, kissed her gently.

"And for Zeb," she murmured.

"And for Zeb," he echoed.

Her hand tightened on his arm. "Will I see you again?" she asked.

"Can't say." He shrugged. "But I'll get word to you. The doc tells me you'll be welcome to stay on here if you like. His wife needs help."

"Maybe," she said. "Especially if you might come back." She offered her lips, a gently, lingering pressure. "Be careful, Fargo," she said. "And thanks for all of it, from the first to the last."

"Stay well, hard nose," he said, left quickly, and strode outside to where the Ovaro waited. He let his thoughts form as he rode through town. Betsy had been right. This was a job that would take some help. Accusations wouldn't do any good. Ben Brookings would lie, be quick to cover his tracks. He might even be tricky enough to lie his way out and stay low until he found another way to begin cheating the government. He had to be nailed down, dead-to-rights, where there'd be no way for him to slip out.

Fargo pushed Brookings aside for the moment. Something else came first, and he headed the Ovaro toward the three wagons that still set quietly at the edge of town.

Will Temple stepped from the Conestoga as he drew to a halt. "You want Ruth?" he asked, and Fargo nodded. The man turned to the wagon, but the tall form had already stepped out, her eyes finding Fargo at once.

"Pack" Fargo growled. "You're leaving with me."

"Where?" Ruth asked, and her eyes were still edged with red.

"I'm giving you a second chance," he said. "That's more than I give most people. Betsy was left for dead because of you. She had things to finish. You're going to take her place."

He watched Ruth's brown eyes hold his, no wavering in them, her chin tilted high. "Fair enough," she said quietly, and he felt a moment of surprise. He'd expected protests, questions at the very least. She went back into the Conestoga and Fargo's glance swept the others as they came from their wagons.

"You're here," he said. "I'll be going back."

"We'll be staying," Will Temple said. "We'll make a place for ourselves."

Fargo's glance held on Charlotte and she slid him a half-smile, came forward, and halted beside him, her voice too low for anyone else to hear. "I'll look in on Betsy," she said.

"That'd be nice," he told her.

"I won't be going back with you, but we'll have memories together," she said.

He let a laugh reach out to her and she turned away. Charlotte would fend well for herself, he was certain. His glance moved to the side as Ruth came from behind the Conestoga leading the horse. She paused at her father and mother, exchanged soft words and embraces, did the same with Hilda Temple, and nodded at the others. The in-charge air was still with her, he saw, but he detected more mask than reality in it now. She climbed onto the horse, cast a cool glance at him, and he turned the Ovaro around and headed south into the Shoshoni Mountains once again. He'd make better time now, he knew. Without the wagons to think about, there were a thousand paths and passages he could use. He chose one covered with harsh mountain grass that led along the side of a ridge, and he rode hard until darkness began to descend. A rock overhang offered a place to bed down and he unsaddled the horses as Ruth brought out a tin of rabbit stew and some johnnycakes.

"Hilda made these last night," she said, and sat in the darkness opposite him as the moon hid behind the crags. "You're going back after Brookings, aren't you?" she asked when they finished the meal.

"You get the cigar."

"It won't be a tea party, I take it," she said.

"Two cigars."

"Don't you think you ought to tell me what you expect of me?" she asked.

"When it's time," he said. "Get some sleep. Every day will be hard riding and hot sun until we get back to Buffalo Corners." He started to undress and she turned away, rose, and took things from her saddlebag, her back to him. She stepped behind a tall boulder and he heard her undressing. He lay all but naked on his bedroll when she returned in the white cotton nightdress. She folded herself on her blanket, her back to him.

"I wish I could take back everything I did," she murmured. "You're never going to believe that, are you?"

"That depends," he said.

"On what?"

"On actions, not words," he growled. "Go to sleep." He turned on his side and drew sleep around himself as the warm night winds became a soft, invisible blanket.

When morning came Fargo woke first, rose, and saw she had turned on her back. The nightgown had crept up to reveal one lovely, long leg, and the modest breasts swelled up over the edge of the neckline. In sleep, the imposed severity in her face was gone and a classic loveliness took its place. He used his canteen, sparingly washed and dressed, and left his shirt off as she woke, blinked, and quickly smoothed the nightgown down over her leg. He walked out from beneath the overhang, scanned the terrain as she dressed, and returned when she'd finished to saddle the Ovaro. He saw her eyes linger on the power and beauty of his torso as he swung into the saddle.

"Stay close," he said, and put the Ovaro into a trot. He kept to narrow passages as much as he could, partly because they offered shade, partly because they offered protection from Shoshoni scouting parties. He rode hard, stopping only once where a thin trickle of water dropped from a rocky perch. He let the horses slowly take in the cooling liquid and finally set off again. The mountain range was as dry and arid as when they'd crossed with the wagons, though he took a completely different route. When the day ended, he pulled the horses into a spot between two junipers.

Ruth slid from the saddle and he saw her face was flushed and shiny with perspiration. Strands of hair had come down to fall across her forehead, and her lips parted as she drew in deep breaths.

"You look better than you do most times," Fargo said.

"Sarcasm?" she returned.

"Truth," he said. "You look real."

"Instead of what?"

"Instead of somebody busy playing a role." He saw her eyes narrow for a moment, anger in their brown depths, but she turned away in silence.

"I'm too tired to eat," she said, took her things, and went behind the rocks. He had three strips of cold beef jerky waiting for her when she returned. "I told you I'm too tired to eat."

"You're not eating for pleasure. You're eating so you'll have strength enough to keep riding," he said.

She sat down, chewed on the jerky, and washed it down with water from her canteen. He watched her practically collapse on her blanket. She was asleep in minutes, and he undressed, feeling the ache in his own body as he stretched out. They had made both time and distance. They were doing well. He couldn't have driven Betsy or Charlotte at the pace he had her. Ruth Temple had inner steel, and that was different than simply being hard-nosed. He closed his eyes and slept until the new day dawned.

Once again, he rode almost without stopping, cutting through the low passages of the high land and refusing to bow to the burning heat.

"I've very little water left, Fargo," Ruth said when they stopped for the night.

"We'll find some tomorrow," he told her.

"Don't feed me lies. I'm not a child," she snapped.

"Still thorny, aren't you?" he grunted. "What makes you think I'm lying to you?"

"What makes you think we'll find water tomorrow?" she tossed back.

"I saw more junipers. That means water's flowing someplace. Maybe underground passages. That often happens. But underground passages always surface someplace," he said.

She lay down, her back to him again. "I'm sorry," she murmured. "I should've known better."

"Yep," he said cheerfully, and she turned to throw a glare at him. " 'Night," he said, and lay back on his bedroll. Once again he was tired but satisfied. They were moving quickly through the mountains. Ben Brookings was drawing closer.

When morning dawned hot and dry, he glimpsed a flight of waxwings and followed. The pursuit led through a long passage that curved downward between sandstone formations. The stone grew higher, the sides steeper, and the passage became wide enough for only single-file riding. He reached the bottom to see the small pond, a circle of cold, deep blue in the arid surroundings, fed by an underground spring.

Ruth pushed up behind him, let out a squeak of delight as she saw the water, and slid from her horse at once. She started to unbutton her shirt and halted, turned to look at him.

"There's a flat rock up there that'll let me see any Shoshoni coming this way," he said. "I'll stand guard while you go in and you can do the same for me."

"Yes, of course," she said, and waited as he dismounted, pulled himself up on the rocks until he reached the flat stone. He sank down on one knee and looked out over the rocky terrain. "But you can see right down here, too." Ruth frowned.

"I can," he agreed.

"And you'll look, of course," she said.

"I will," he said. She frowned up at him and he

160

smiled back. "You're wasting time," he said, and she turned, took a towel from her saddlebag, and put it around her shoulders. With the towel around her, she shed skirt and underclothes, then her blouse, and stepped into the pool as she flung the towel aside. He got only a glimpse of a nicely curved back and white, square shoulders. "Good job," he said and watched her as she paddled in the deep, cool pool, dived, washed, and swam to where a small bubble of water surfaced from the underground spring. She did all of it without showing more than bare arms and shoulders and an occasional flash of calf.

His eyes moved from Ruth to the rocks and back again. He watched as she swam to the edge of the pool, reached out, and drew the towel to her. She held it up as she came out, wrapped it around herself, and stayed entirely modest and proper.

He swept the distant rocks again. Nothing moved but a chuckwalla, and he clambered down. "Your turn," he said. "You can dry off while you're up there."

She brushed past him and he admired the backs of her legs as she started up the rocks. He waited for her to reach the flat lookout place before he threw off clothes and dived naked into the pool. He knew her eyes were on him as his powerful, muscled body cleaved the water with hardly a ripple. The welcome coolness flowed over him, soothing and exciting, like the touch of a woman, and he turned on his back, floated on the surface. He glanced up at Ruth and she turned away at once, gazed out over the rocks, and he smiled, turned, and dived deep into the cold bottom of the pool, surfaced, and shook away water as he climbed onto the hot stones that edged the pool. He lay down on his back and seemed to close his eyes.

Through slitted lids, he saw Ruth look down at him, her eyes taking in every inch of his body. He stayed motionless and felt the sun quickly drying his skin. Ruth cast a quick glance across the rocks and returned her eyes to him. He waited a few minutes longer, and his eyes still seemingly closed, he called up to her.

"You're supposed to be watching for Shoshoni," he said, and heard her gasp of embarrassment as she turned her eyes out to the rocks. He laughed, sat up, and began to pull on clothes as she kept her eyes out across the terrain. "You can come down now," he said as he finished dressing, and he waited as she began to carefully clamber down the rocks, keeping the towel in place with one hand. He swung onto the pinto when she reached bottom. "I'll wait for you at the other end of the passage," he said, and caught the tiny frown as she peered at him. He sent the horse on through the crevice of rock, emerged onto a plateau with a thick stand of juniper growing along one side. He waited and Ruth came along in but a few minutes to swing alongside him.

"You always do the unexpected, don't you?" she said. "Like riding off to let me dress like a perfect gentleman."

"You surprised or disappointed?" he tossed at her.

He expected a sharp, disapproving reply but instead he saw her think for a long minute. "I don't know," she said.

"My compliments," he answered.

"On what?"

"Honesty," he said. "It comes hard when you're

new at it." There was no edge to his words, and her face stayed sober.

"Yes," she said very quietly. "Yes." She fell silent and he led the way into the junipers, rode in the shade of the trees, and when night came, they were in the low range where the gambel oaks replaced the junipers and the land grew less arid.

He found a glen and made camp. The moon had taken on more substance and laid a silvered glow over the glen. He set out his bedroll, pulled off his shirt and gun belt, and waited for Ruth to get up and go into the trees to change. He felt the tiny furrow creep across his forehead as she sat up, reached hands to her hair, and undid clasps; brown tresses cascaded loose and full around her face. It was a kind of magic, he reflected, the way it turned hardness into softness, severity into warmth. The furrow grew deeper as he saw her fingers undo buttons and she got to her feet, made quick motions at the waistband of her skirt, and the garment fell at her feet. She flung off shirt, pushed down pink bloomers all in one quick motion, and stood before him, absolutely nude in the pale-silver light.

He took in modest breasts that were beautifully cupped, small dark-pink nipples on each surrounded by a circle of amber pink. Strong, square shoulders held the breasts high and firm, and a narrow, long waist flowed into flat, wide hips, a flat belly, and beneath it, a modest triangle that spread out wide at the top edges and tapered sharply to disappear into the V of long, lovely legs, thighs that curved slowly, and long calves that were an echo of the upper limbs. He felt himself responding to the sight of her, rising, pushing, and he lay back, yanked off clothes, and let himself throb upwards. But Ruth stayed motionless in front of him, as though she were suddenly rooted in place. He reached up, curled his hands around the cup of each breast. She gave a sharp cry and fell forward onto him, her arms clasped around his neck.

Her mouth pressed on his, seeking, demanding, her lips opened, her tongue a darting, probing, hungering invitation. "Take me," Ruth breathed between kisses. "Oh, God, take me." She wriggled her body, pushed upward, and almost drove one modest breast into his mouth. He took the soft offering, drew in the firm, pink nipple, and sucked on it. Ruth screamed in delight. She tore away from his lips, half-fell, half-threw herself onto her back, and pulled him with her. Again, as his warm, throbbing maleness came against her belly, she shrieked, and her hands came up to cup his face. "Take me, Fargo. Don't listen to anything I say. Just take me, oh, please, please," she gasped out, and he pressed his mouth over her breast, let his hand trace a slow, sulfurous path down the hollows of the long, slim body.

He pushed through the wiry nap of the tapering triangle, felt the small mound beneath it, and Ruth's hands dug into him and her thighs suddenly slapped hard against each other. "No," she cried out. "No, no, no."

He paused and her words came to him, and he pushed downward again to the dark apex of the triangle. Her thighs stayed clamped together. "No, no, no," He pushed his fingers deeper, in between her thighs. "Oh, no, oh," she gasped, but he continued to push and felt his maleness eagerly throbbing, searching. He let his hand push harder, grew rough, and her thighs fell open and closed again instantly. But his fingers were touching the slippery, lubricious lips, caressing, stroking. "Ah, ah . . . eeeeiiii, oh, no, no, no," Ruth half-screamed.

He pushed deeper, stroked slowly, and with a cry that seemed to tear from the depths of her soul, her legs fell open, came up, closed behind his buttocks. He lifted, brought his thrusting organ over her, and slid forward, the world suddenly made only of warm, wet ecstasy, flesh enclosing flesh, the rod and the staff of pure sensual delight.

"No, no, no," Ruth cried out as she arched her back to take him more deeply inside her. He drew back, thrust forward, quickly found the rhythm for her, and she moved with him, her mouth biting at his chest, pressed against his own nipples as her hands clasped around his neck. She lifted her breasts and he took one and then the other while he felt the spiral suddenly growing inside him. Ruth felt the pull of it, too, and her hips began to almost leap up and down, back and forth. He felt the contractions of the luscious walls around him and stopped holding back, let himself explode with her, and her cry became a long, wailing sound that rose into the night, hung in midair, and finally broke off with a shuddered sob.

She fell back, her breasts rising high with each deep breath, and her thighs still quivered around him until finally she lay still, only her hands moving up and down his chest. She turned to him finally, pushed up on one elbow, and the round cups of her breasts rested against his chest. "Not bad for a prune, was it?"

"Not bad at all," he said. "Why, now? Why not back at the pool?"

"Honesty comes hard, you said. It also comes slow," she answered. "Or maybe I just suddenly realized there might not be another night, another time. We're getting close, I know that." She put her head down on his chest, and her voice seemed as if from far away. "And maybe part of it was wanting to make you believe me. You said it would take actions, not words," she murmured.

His hand moved down her back, across the small, tight rear, reached down to the dark and still-moist places. "You want to try convincing me some more?" he asked, and she lifted her head at once and her lips reached for his.

"Yes, oh, yes," she said. She came to him quickly, letting her own hands explore, caress, excite, and again he paid no attention to the denials and protests that still cried out from a past time. When her scream of fulfillment rose into the night stillness, she clung to him, stayed tight against him as she finally fell asleep, and when the new day dawned, she was still wrapped around his body. He gently moved her legs from around his and she murmured in protest before she blinked her eyes open.

"Time to move on, Ruth," he said.

"Ruthie," she murmured, and shook her brown hair. She detached herself from him with a quick roll, turned, and watched him pull on clothes. When he finished, she began to dress and he found a small stream nearby. They ate wild plums, and his eyes peered down at the low hills.

"We'll make Buffalo Corners by tonight," he said.

"And then?"

"Time for another kind of convincing," he said, and she nodded gravely. "I'll fill you in while we ride," he said, and she climbed onto her mount to come alongside him. She listened without interruption as he told her what Betsy had learned. When he finished, she cast a quizzical glance his way.

"How do you expect to get him dead-to-rights?" she asked.

"We're going to pay two visits in town after dark. If Brookings hauls all this army contract freight, there had to be an army command post nearby," he said. "I'm going to pay a call there."

"The other visit?" Ruth asked.

"To the general store to get some boy's clothes that'll fit you," he said, and put the pinto into a fast trot. The ride down through the foothills was fast and without trouble, but night had come when they reached Buffalo Corners.

"Just as well," he muttered. "I don't want any of Brookings' men recognizing either of us, especially you." He found the army command post on the far edge of the town, a supply-and-storage depot with a high wood stockade fence. The sergeant at arms gave him trouble, and Fargo fastened the soldier with a cold stare. "I know it's late and I'm sure the captain doesn't see anybody at this hour, but he'll see me," Fargo said.

"Why the hell will he see you?" the soldier blurted.

"Because I'm going to make him into a general," Fargo said. "And I'm going to make you into a shit-shoveling stable boy if you don't get him."

The soldier stared back, frowned, debated, and read the strength in the big man's eyes. "Wait here," he muttered, and disappeared into the officers' quarters. He returned and led the way into a neat, square office where a man with graying hair and a sharply pressed uniform rose from behind a desk.

"Captain Stebbins," he said with a nod and a half-bow to Ruth. "The sergeant tells me you've a forceful approach," he said to Fargo. "And I do want to meet a man who's going to make me into a general."

"Guaranteed," Fargo said. "The army's being cheated out of tens of thousands of dollars every year. An officer who puts a stop to that can count on becoming a general."

"I'm listening," the captain said as he sat down.

Fargo told him what he knew in quick, terse sentences, and Ruth backed up his story about Betsy's Uncle Zeb. When he finished, the captain stared back with incredulousness a wreath around his face.

"This is preposterous. Ben Brookings is a respected man, under contract to haul for the government for years," he said.

"And he's been stealing for years," Fargo said.

"I can't go on just words. You come in here with a wild story like that and expect me to accuse the man. I can't do it," Capt. Stebbins said.

"Don't expect you to," Fargo said. "You have a shipment going out soon?"

"Tomorrow, wheat and barley," the captain said. "Brookings Haulage will be carrying it, as always. And two of the army's men will check it through when it reaches Andersonville."

"The two Brookings pays off," Fargo said.

"More words. I'd need hard proof, mister, very hard proof," the captain said.

"You be in Andersonville when that shipment arrives. Stay in the background, but be there. I'll give you proof," Fargo said.

The captain thought for a long moment and returned his gaze to the big man in front of him, took in Ruth with a sweeping glance. "There's only one reason I'm going to do this," he said finally. "I don't think you could make up a story as wild as this, and I don't see any reason why you'd do so." He rose to his feet, his face growing stern. "I'll be in Andersonville. If you don't come up with hard proof, you can both count on being guests of the United States Army."

"I'll see you in Andersonville," Fargo said, and took Ruth's elbow as he left.

Outside, she frowned at him. "You still haven't told me just how you intend to nail Brookings," she said.

"Keep the faith, honey," he said. "Now let's get you some clothes. A hat's important, a ten-gallon hat. Don't forget that." He waited outside as Ruth woke the owner of the general store and with a combination of charm and insistence got him to open up for her. When she returned, she carried shirt, trousers, and a wide-brimmed black hat in her arms.

"I told him they were for my young brother and he was about my size," she said as they rode out of town. He found a place to bed down and she slept in his arms until the morning dawned.

"Been wanting you to put your hair down, and now that you've done it, I want you to put it up again," he said. She laughed as she quickly pulled the brown hair back severely, tied it into a bun, and was finished in moments.

"Practice," she said, and pulled on the boy's trousers and shirt. She put on the hat when she finished, and he eyed her carefully. Her straight nose and clean chin let her easily pass for a boy in his teens.

"Just keep the damn hat on," he said as they rode toward town. He halted on a hillock that let him look down at the army storage depot. The wait was short as he saw the wagon roll out of the stockade gate, a tarpaulin covering the sacks of grain inside. A long, dead-axle Owensboro dray with high sides, it bore the letters BROOKINGS HAULAGE in gold paint.

Fargo took in the two men on the wagon as they sat side by side on the wide driver's seat. "Just as Betsy said, a driver and helper," he murmured. "We'll hang back and stay on high ground." He sent the Ovaro up into a line of oaks that more or less ran along the path of the road below, and he kept the horses in the trees as the wagon rolled unhurriedly, the two horses heavy hauling animals—Clydesdales interbred with domestic stock, he guessed.

He let most of the morning go by and saw the wagon make a long, slow curve southward, move into country with good tree cover.

"It's time," he said to Ruth. "You ride down, come at them from the front. Move slowly, let them see you. Ask them the way to Andersonville when you stop. I want their attention on you while I circle around behind them."

"Yes, sir," she said, and he smiled as she dropped her voice at least one octave.

"Get going. This'll be the easy part." He wheeled the Ovaro around, cut back, and moved down toward the road below. He stayed in the trees and saw Ruth approach the wagon. The driver's helper brought a rifle out at once, Fargo saw, kept it trained on the figure riding up to the wagon. Fargo moved the Ovaro forward, still stayed in the trees as he neared the dray from the rear.

Ruth had halted and he heard the two men talking to her as he drew the Colt, pulled the pinto out of the trees a few scant yards from the back of the big dray.

"Drop the rifle," he said, and saw the two men

stiffen. "Hurry up about it," he added, his tone growing sharp.

The man let the rifle fall and the gun clattered onto the front wheel of the wagon and fell to the ground. Fargo saw Ruth bend low in the saddle and scoop the gun up as he pulled the Ovaro forward. He came alongside the driver, reached over, and took the man's six-gun from his holster. "Now get down, both of you," he said, and both men slowly climbed from the wagon.

"We're carryin' grain, not gold," the driver said.

"I know," Fargo said as he swung the pinto, the Colt trained on the two men.

"Who the hell hijacks grain?" The man frowned.

"I like buckwheat cakes," Fargo said, and gestured to Ruth. "Either of them moves a finger, shoot them," he said as he took his lariat and holstered the Colt. He tied the men with rope and knots they'd need a week to undo, dragged them deep into the woods, and secured them to separate trees.

"You can't leave us here. Nobody'll ever find us," the driver protested as Fargo took the loading weight sheet from him.

"I'll send somebody for you." Fargo smiled. "You just have yourselves a nice rest." He trotted back to the wagon, tethered the pinto behind it, and saw Ruth had already done so with her mount. "Let's go," he said as he climbed up on the high driver's seat and took the reins. "We don't want to keep anybody waiting."

Fargo snapped the reins and the horses responded, increased speed until he'd made up time, then he slowed the team. He estimated they'd rolled along the road for at least an hour when, as he rounded a slow curve, he saw the three horsemen waiting at the roadside. A thick cluster of hackberry rose up behind them and he pulled the big dray to a halt.

One of the men, heavy-faced, with a surly expression, moved closer. "Where's Harrison and Green?" he asked.

"Too much rotgut last night. We had to take over for them," Fargo said. "Name's Swanson. This is Tom Hodd."

The man eyed them, debated, grumbled. "Brookings should've got word to us," he said.

"Guess he didn't have time," Fargo said.

The man grunted and waved his arm in the air, and the brush by the hackberry parted as a smaller wagon rolled out, a converted dry-goods wagon with closed sides and special heavy wheels and axles. One man drove and another rode at his side on horseback. He wheeled the smaller wagon alongside the big dray and the others dismounted, pulled the tarpaulin back from the sacks, and begun to transfer every other sack out of the dray. They worked quickly, rearranged the sacks they left in the dray, and when they'd taken what they wanted, they pulled the tarpaulin back in place and shut the doors of the closed van. They'd transferred about a third of the shipment, Fargo estimated, and he exchanged a quick glance with Ruth as she sat, face lowered, under the big hat.

"All set," Fargo said as he picked up the reins and glanced at the heavy-faced man.

The man frowned as he stared back. "Harrison and Green always helped load," the man growled.

Fargo shrugged. "Guess you'll be glad when they're back," he said.

The man's eyes continued to bore into him. "They

didn't bring extra horses along with them, either. No damn need for extra horses," he said.

Fargo shrugged again. "Nobody told us that," he said.

"That Ovaro. I've seen that horse," the man said, and Fargo cursed silently.

"There's more than one around," he remarked, and lifted the reins to snap them over the team.

"Not like that one," the man said, his voice rising. "Shit, I know where I saw him." Fargo saw the man reach for his gun, the others looking on, still taken with surprise. "Blast them," the man said as he yanked his six-gun out.

Fargo's Colt leapt from the holster with the speed of a cougar's attack as he lunged sideways, knocked Ruth down across the driver's seat. Lying half atop her, he fired over her head, and the man bucked in his saddle, twisted, and fell. But Fargo had swung the Colt, fired again, and two of the others went down. The driver on the smaller wagon dropped the reins as he cringed. "Don't shoot, mister. You win," he shouted, and Fargo had the gun barrel trained on the last man in the saddle. The man stared at the others where they lay on the ground, and raised his hands in the air. Fargo pushed himself up to a sitting position and pulled Ruth up with him. Her hat fell off and he saw the two men stare at her. "Damn," the one breathed.

"Drop your guns, nice and easy," Fargo said, and climbed down from the dray. The men obeyed and he used his lariat to tie them together, bound them tight, and put them inside the smaller wagon. He bound their ankles and pushed them down onto the grain sacks, closed the doors, and locked them with a key that dangled from the latch.

"Pull it back into the trees," he told Ruth, and she drove the wagon into the high brush and hid it in the shadows of the thick foliage as he pulled the lifeless forms off the road. "Can't ever be too careful," he said, climbed back onto the big dray, and sent the wagon rolling forward. Ruth pulled her ten-gallon hat back hard over her head and sat close to him.

When Andersonville came into sight and the day began to slip to a close, he nudged her with his elbow. "Move over," he said. "Helpers don't cuddle up to the drivers, least none that I know."

She moved to the other end of the driver's seat, put one foot up on the rail and hunched forward. "This better?" she asked.

"For now." He laughed. He peered ahead as he rolled into Andersonville and saw it was a sizable town with a good number of long-haul, six-team outfits lined up along the main street. As he neared the center of town, he spotted a half-dozen small, one-horse army spring wagons. The town was plainly a place where supplies were hauled in and taken off to different command posts. He saw two wagons slowing ahead of him and spotted a knot of figures near a weighing platform. "You take over," he said to Ruth, and drew a glance of instant alarm. "I see Brookings in that damn tan stetson of his," he said as he handed her the loading sheet. "You just drive the wagon up onto that platform weighing scale and give the two army men the weight sheet. I'll do the rest."

He slid sideways, dropped from the wagon, and trotted around to the far side of it. Staying in a crouch, he moved along with the dray, lifted his head enough to see that Brookings was in casual conversation with a portly man in a green frock coat.

Fargo stayed behind the wagon as Ruth drove onto the long platform scale, and he fell back, dropped to one knee as the two army men came up to her. She handed one the loading weight sheet.

"You're late," the corporal muttered, and she shrugged.

Fargo watched the second soldier peer at the numbers on the scale at the end of the platform, step over to the first one, who showed him the loading weight sheet.

"Right on the nose," the soldier said. "Move off."

Fargo, on one knee to the side, saw Brookings suddenly break off his conversation and push forward, a frown on his heavy-jawed face.

"Wait a minute," he said as he came toward the wagon still on the scale. "Where the hell's Harrison and Green?" he asked as he exchanged glances with the two soldiers. They shrugged and he stepped toward Ruth.

"They're tied up. They couldn't come," Fargo said as he rose.

Brookings spun, astonishment on his face. He reached for his gun as he saw the big man and put the message, if not the words, together.

Fargo drew the Colt out, firing before Brookings' gun cleared its holster. His shot sent the gun spinning into the air and Brookings clutched at his hand as he stepped backward.

"Son of a bitch," Brookings snarled, charged forward, and Fargo saw him draw a small pocket pistol from his vest.

Fargo's long arm shot out, his fist slamming into the man's jaw, and Brookings went down, the little pistol falling to the ground. Fargo cast a quick glance at the two soldiers. Both men had stepped back, uncertainty on their faces. Brookings pushed himself to his feet and Fargo crashed a looping right against the man's jaws and Brookings went down again.

"For Zeb Wills," Fargo said, stepped forward, waiting as Brookings staggered to his feet. He sidestepped a wavering lunge, seized the man by the shoulders, lifted, and slammed him facedown onto the weighing platform. He heard the splintering of nose and cheekbones as Brookings hit the hard wood of the scale. "That one's for Betsy," he said to the quivering form that moaned through the stream of blood from his face.

Fargo lifted his eyes, speared the two soldiers. "No trouble, mister," one said.

"At least you've enough brains for that," Fargo said. He glanced to his left and saw the blue uniform with the captain's bars on the shoulders come forward, two rifle-carrying troopers alongside him. "Hello, General." Fargo grinned.

"Take those men into custody," the officer said to the two soldiers with him.

"You check the weight of that load again and you'll find it about a third light," Fargo said. "You'll find the rest of the grain about ten miles from here in a converted dry-goods wagon."

The captain motioned and a half-dozen more soldiers appeared. "Take that man to the doctor and put him under arrest," he said with a nod to Brookings, who still lay facedown on the loading scale. "I'll get his statement later." He turned to Fargo and put his hand out. "I'll see that you are given a commendation for this," he said. "You going to take my troopers back to the other wagon?"

"No need to. They'll find it inside a thick spread of hackberry right alongside the road," Fargo said.

"My helper and I have some celebrating to do." He looked up at Ruth and she threw the ten-gallon hat into the air and swung from the wagon.

"Yes," she said as she untied the horses and climbed into the saddle. "The army isn't the only one that can give commendations."

Capt. Stebbins let a slow smile cross his face. "I'd exchange one of yours for one of ours anyday," he said.

"Me, too," Fargo agreed, and pulled himself onto the Ovaro. He waved at the blue-uniformed figure as he rode away, Ruth alongside him. He cast a glance at Ruth as she shook her head and the brown hair came loose to fall around her face. "You did well," he said.

"I'm going to do even better," she returned, and the unsaid promise danced in her brown eyes.

Fargo put the pinto into a gallop and headed for the green lush woods.

## LOOKING FORWARD!

**The following is the opening
section from the next novel in the exciting
*Trailsman* series from Signet:**

## THE TRAILSMAN #62
## HORSETHIEF CROSSING

*1861—San Antonio, Texas*

The girl winked at him as she closed the door and slowly, deliberately slid the bolt to lock the two of them away from the rest of the world. She smiled in anticipation of a long and languid afternoon. That was fair enough. Skye Fargo was damn sure looking forward to it too.

Beyond the small window the sun was bright and hard, its harsh glare softened by a ragged length of muslin tacked above it. The room was not much, poorly furnished and seldom cleaned.

The girl, however, was something else again. She was as fine as the room was poor. Her hair and eyes were dark and gleaming, the shine of youth and health on her long, loose, raven-black hair, a bright, happy sparkle of mischief and joy showing in her eyes. She wore a peasant blouse, a loose-fitting skirt of homespun, and her legs and feet were bare, but no external trappings could lessen her loveliness. She was young and pretty and found the entire world full of joy.

With another wink and a short peal of irrepressible laughter that exposed tiny white teeth set against a dusky, matte-satin complexion, she reached high, having to rise on her tiptoes to give Fargo a brief kiss. Then quickly she began to peel out of her clothes.

Fargo began just as quickly to pull off his shirt. He kicked his boots off and let them drop unheeded into a corner of the little room.

He was a handsome man, a full head taller than the girl and with the lean-hipped, broad-shouldered build of the born horseman. His hair was near as dark as hers but his lake-blue eyes were not so merry. Even in this moment of anticipated pleasures, there was a measure of reserve about him, a caution born of far trails and constant dangers.

He set a short, blunt Sharps carbine into a corner and unbuckled his gun belt to hang the Colt on the bedpost before he slid his trousers down and stood naked before the girl.

It had taken her only moments to undress. She was even lovelier now than he had expected, her breasts not overlarge but standing firm and proud and dark-tipped. Her legs were nicely formed if a trifle short for the rest of her fine frame. Her belly was nearly flat, soft and smooth, and only very slightly convex. Her pubic hair was a thick, curly patch of promise.

She smiled again and Fargo held his arms open. She ran forward into them, and he held her close, the heat of his erection trapped between their bodies. He kissed her, having to lift her so that her feet dangled inches off the floor in order to make that contact. She laughed and explored his mouth hungrily with her tongue and mobile lips. Her mouth was exceptionally soft and her breath clean and tasting faintly of mint.

Fargo reached low, sliding his hand down her hip in a slow caress, and turned her in his arms so that he could put a forearm behind her knees and lift her. With another laugh she locked her arms behind his neck and began to kiss his throat.

He carried her the few steps to the bed and sat with her in his lap, his cock pressing against her buttocks. She wriggled, deliberately exciting him all the further, and was pleased with what she could see in his eyes.

Fargo cupped her right breast in his hand. It was firm and elastic, her flesh flowing in his fingers like moist clay, delightfully warm and sweet clay. He bent and took her nipple into his mouth, rolling it on his tongue and eliciting a sigh of pleasure from her.

She shifted off his lap and lay beside him so that she could touch and stroke and fondle him. Fargo offered no objection.

He nipped lightly at her other nipple with his lips and, carefully, with his teeth, and she sighed again.

"Love me, Fargo. Please love me now."

Love. She meant it too. For Margarita this was no commercial exchange. There was nothing tawdry or sordid about it. For this delightful girl it truly was a matter of loving, one that she enjoyed and was pleased to give.

She opened herself to his touch, and she was already moistly eager for him. Tiny pearls of dewy wetness beaded the curling hairs that surrounded her opening. He slid a finger into her, surprised at the resistance he encountered there. Certainly not of any reluctance but the tightness of youth and perhaps even of relative inexperience.

He covered her, and she wrapped him in her arms and her legs and opened herself wide to welcome and receive him.

He had been right. She was extraordinarily tight, trapping him deep inside her body and surrounding him with damp heat.

"Let me?" she whispered.

He nodded and held himself braced rigid above her. And rigid as well within her.

Margarita began to move her hips, raising and lowering herself slowly, impaling herself. She shivered and shuddered with the pleasure of it as alternately he filled her and then was withdrawn almost to the point of losing contact with her.

Fargo didn't move at all. Margarita was doing more than enough for both of them. Her breathing quickened and so did her motion until she was pumping her hips wildly beneath him.

She bucked and plunged, arching her neck, full lips drawn back from her teeth and eyes unfocused.

"Ah . . . ah . . . *ahhhh!*"

Fargo could feel the gather and rise of his own pleasure deep in his groin, spreading, filling him. The intense sensation drawn from the most distant parts of his body and flowing together in one concentrated rush that poured out of his balls, swelled his shaft to overflowing, and burst out of his body and into hers.

He shuddered and stiffened and only in that last wild, uncontrolled moment plunged forward, throwing his weight onto and into her.

Margarita clutched at him fiercely, arms and legs alike clamping hard around him, pulling him to her, pulling him into her greedily as the last convulsive shudderings of her own release turned into the joy of sharing his release.

She sighed and went limp beneath him. Fargo kissed her gently and lay for a time on top of her, his lean body pillowed on her smaller, softer length, his satiated member limp and wet but still deep inside her. Her breathing slowed, and after a moment he rolled off her and Margarita nestled close against him, unwilling to give up the contact with this darkly handsome *norteamericano*.

Far below and half a world away—or so it seemed at that moment—a piano tinkled faintly and voices were raised in laughter.

Fargo had stopped in at the saloon only for a beer to cut the dust of travel. He'd found something far finer than anything that could be created by man. He rolled his head on the pillow to look into the wide, happy eyes of the girl and bent just enough to kiss the tip of her nose. Her upper lip wrinkled, and she sneezed.

"Was that . . .? No, couldn't be. Let me try it again." He kissed her there again, and she sneezed again. Both of them laughed. He rolled onto his side and pulled her to him for a proper kiss this time. Her breasts were warm and firm against his chest. She'd been thoroughly satisfied but certainly not satiated. His kiss aroused her again. He could feel it in the change in her breathing, the slight quickening of it, and in the way she rubbed her hands up and down the hard planes of his back.

"Again? Yes?" She sounded immeasurably pleased by the idea.

"Again. Yes," he confirmed.

"You want me to help you?"

Before he could answer, Margarita disentangled herself from his arms and shifted low so that the ends of her hair trailed lazily across his belly.

She took him into her mouth and began to bob her head slowly up and down.

Far, far away, somewhere out in the glare of the sunlight, there was a rattle of small explosions. Gunfire. Heavy pistols, Fargo judged. Not that he cared at the moment.

Margarita stopped what she was doing and looked toward the window with wide, frightened eyes.

She looked damn cute like that, Fargo thought, with the head of his pecker clamped, but for the moment forgotten, between those pretty lips.

The fear that he could see in her eyes, though, wasn't cute at all. He stroked the back of her head. "Are you all right?"

She shuddered and pulled away from him, sitting up on the bed and hugging her arms tight around herself.

"The guns, they . . . I have seen bad things, Fargo. So many bad things. I am sorry."

"It's all right, honey. We aren't in any hurry." He smiled at her reassuringly. "Will it make you feel any better if I take a look? Make sure nothing's wrong?"

She nodded quickly. Too quickly. She looked nervous.

He kissed her and said, "It'll be all right. I won't let anything or anyone hurt you. I promise."

As if to make him out a liar, there was another hard rattle of gunfire from the street below. It sounded closer this time. Margarita turned her face away from the window and squeezed her eyes shut. She was pale and trembling.

Fargo petted her again and went to the window. He raised the scrap of muslin and looked down at the street.

From where he now was he couldn't see what the excitemnt was all about, but the people down below could. They were looking off toward Fargo's left at something. A few were running for shelter. Others stood rooted where they were, spectating with open mouths and uncomprehending blank looks.

More gunshots sounded from the left, and across the street a man wearing a necktie and sleeve garters rushed out onto the sidewalk with a brace of old, large-caliber horse pistols.

A group of hard-charging riders—five, six of them—dashed into view to the left of Fargo's window. The storekeeper across the way raised one of his pistols and fired at them, hitting no one. He dropped the single-shot weapon and shifted the other to his right hand for another shot. The riders were virtually beneath Fargo's window now.

The storekeeper took aim. Three of the men on

horseback turned their revolvers toward the man. They fired, and one bullet caught the man low in the stomach, buckling him forward. His finger squeezed involuntarily on the trigger of the huge pistol, and the weapon belched flame and lead.

The unaimed shot caught a horse in the side of the head, dropping the animal into the dust of the street and spilling its rider.

The other men on horseback saw and wheeled, sending a shower of bullets down the street. One of them rode over to the storekeeper and made sure of him by sending a final slug into the back of his skull.

"Bastards," Fargo muttered.

The man who was down was trapped, his left foot caught by the weight of the carcass. He kicked and struggled and finally pulled himself free, his foot coming out bare except for a tattered sock. His boot remained under the dead horse.

Fargo expected the others to pick him up and ride double for their getaway. Instead, when he tried to mount behind the saddle of the nearest rider, the mounted man pushed him away and snapped something that Fargo couldn't hear through the glasss of the window.

The downed man nodded and looked wildly about.

Then he ran wildly toward the best horse he could see.

"Oh, shit!" Fargo snarled.

The son of a bitch was headed toward the black-and-white Ovaro tied in front of the saloon, directly beneath the window where Fargo stood watching.

"No!" Fargo bellowed, knowing even as he said it that if the man could hear it would have no effect.

Fargo dashed across the small room and grabbed his Colt.

By the time he got back to the window the son of a bitch had the reins of the Ovaro free from the hitch rail. He vaulted into Fargo's saddle, and the Ovaro balked and curvetted.

Fargo snatched the muslin away from the window and tried to pull the window open. The damn thing was stuck.

He was in no humor to take time wrestling with it. He smashed the glass with the barrel of the Colt and quickly knocked the sharp shards of clinging glass away.

The falling glass got the attention of the men down below. They looked up and one of them fired, his bullet thudding into the wall just to the right of the window frame and ripping through the thin wood to send a shower of splinters into the room.

Fargo fired. The bastard on the Ovaro flinched. Fargo wasn't sure, but he thought he had hit him. How hard was another question.

One of the other riders grabbed the reins of the fidgety pinto, and the six of them bolted once again toward the right.

Fargo took aim on the back of the rider who was leading the Ovaro. He sighted carefully between and just below the shoulder blades. If he could knock that one out of the saddle, the pinto might stop where it was rather than join the rush of horses.

"Please, no!"

He felt his arm being dragged down just as he applied pressure on the trigger, and his shot went low, spending itself harmlessly in the dirt behind the heels of the retreating horses but sending up a spray of small gravel that only served to speed them along.

One of the riders threw a snap shot over his shoulder in Fargo's general direction. Fargo had no idea where that one went.

Down the block to the left more guns were firing now. The riders bent low and raked their horses with their spurs.

"Dammit, woman, leave me be." Fargo shook himself free of Margarita's panicky clinging and shoved her rudely away.

He spun back to the window with the Colt raised.

He was too late.

The horseman swept around a corner and out of sight, leaving only dust and confusion behind them.

"Damn," Fargo groaned.

He was pissed. The girl was cowering at his feet, arms wrapped around his bare calves, crying, grabbing at him for whatever comfort and security he might have been able to offer for her terror.

He could see her fear and he was sorry for that, but he had no time for her right now.

He rushed toward the door, then remembered that he was bare-ass naked and had to grab up his clothing.

By the time he had his trousers on, he realized the futility of it. Those men were mounted. One of them on the finest horse Fargo had ever seen, dammit. On Fargo's own Ovaro. Dammit.

There was no way he was going to catch them on foot.

Hopeless, he went back to the window.

A hurriedly assembled posse went thundering past,

raising dust and hell but probably apt to raise little in the way of results.

The damn-fool townsmen hadn't taken time to prepare for a long chase. They rode in whatever clothing they had happened to be wearing at the time, and he could see no provisions or bedrolls tied behind their cantles.

They would be back soon, he figured. And empty-handed.

"Oh, hell," Fargo mumbled. He sat on the edge of the bed and took his time about getting his boots on and finishing dressing.

The girl was still huddled naked and miserable on the dirty floor of the bare little room, but he made no attempt to comfort or to reassure her now.

Skye Fargo felt too empty at the sudden loss of the Ovaro to think about anything or anyone else right now. He looked toward the window, toward the unseen and now-distant riders, and the look he sent after them would have chilled the nerves of a rattlesnake.

However far those men went, wherever they tried to hide, the Trailsman figured to find them.

Whatever it took, whatever the cost, whatever the coin, time, or sweat, or blood, he would spend it.